Old Mountains, New Echoes

Ruskin Bond is known for his signature simplistic and witty writing style. He is the author of several bestselling short stories, novellas, collections, essays and children's books; and has contributed a number of poems and articles to various magazines and anthologies. At the age of 23, he won the prestigious John Llewellyn Rhys Prize for his first novel, *The Room on the Roof*. He was also the recipient of the Padma Shri in 1999, Lifetime Achievement Award by the Delhi Government in 2012 and the Padma Bhushan in 2014.

Born in 1934, Ruskin Bond grew up in Jamnagar, Shimla, New Delhi and Dehradun. Apart from three years in the UK, he has spent all his life in India and now lives in Landour, Mussoorie, with his adopted family.

RUSKIN BOND
Old Mountains, New Echoes

RUPA

Published by
Rupa Publications India Pvt. Ltd 2024
7/16, Ansari Road, Daryaganj
New Delhi 110002

Sales centres:
Bengaluru Chennai
Hyderabad Jaipur Kathmandu
Kolkata Mumbai Prayagraj

Copyright © Ruskin Bond 2024

All rights reserved.
This is a work of fiction. Names, characters, places and incidents are either the product of the author's imagination or are used fictitiously and any resemblance to any actual person, living or dead, events or locales is entirely coincidental.

No part of this publication may be reproduced, transmitted, or stored in a retrieval system, in any form or by any means, electronic, mechanical, photocopying, recording or otherwise, without the prior permission of the publisher.

P-ISBN: 978-93-6156-005-7
E-ISBN: 978-93-6156-010-1

First impression 2024

10 9 8 7 6 5 4 3 2 1

The moral right of the author has been asserted.

Printed in India

This book is sold subject to the condition that it shall not, by way of trade or otherwise, be lent, resold, hired out, or otherwise circulated, without the publisher's prior consent, in any form of binding or cover other than that in which it is published.

CONTENTS

Introduction   *vii*

1. The Room on the Roof (An Excerpt)   1
2. Once You Have Lived with Mountains   18
3. The Postman Knocks   21
4. White Clouds, Green Mountains   26
5. My Trees in the Himalayas   30
6. Dust on the Mountain   34
7. Wild Flowers Near a Mountain Stream   54
8. Birdsong in the Hills   57
9. Breakfast at Barog   64
10. Cold Beer at Chhutmalpur   71
11. Sounds I Like to Hear   77
12. Landour Bazaar   81
13. From the Pool to the Glacier   89
14. How Far Is the River?   113

15. A Night Walk Home   117
16. A Village in Garhwal   121
17. The Night the Roof Blew Off   132

INTRODUCTION

Each one of us may have a variety of memories attached to mountains. For some, it might be an escape from the monotonous life of the cities. While for others, like me, it is home. Whether you are there briefly or for a long time, mountains leave an everlasting impact. If you take a walk along the steep, uneven path of the mountains, you might get lost in the swards of flowers and ferns, in the company of deodars or in the ghostly tales carried down from generations.

The stories in *Old Mountains, New Echoes* explore the varied ways in which we cherish life in the mountains. Tales like 'Cold Beer at Chhutmalpur' and 'Breakfast at Barog' speak of the joy and adventure of travelling to the mountains. Other tales like 'My Trees in the Himalayas' and 'Wild Flowers Near a Mountain Stream' speak of the delights one might come across while living in the mountains. Further, stories like 'A Village in Garhwal' and 'Landour Bazaar' give you a peek into the slow yet lively pulse of life in hill stations.

There is a new experience waiting around every corner, if you choose to look for it, in the twists and turns of the hills. Whether it is the familiarity of old mountains that you miss, or the echoes of new experiences that invite you to the hills—I hope the endeared stories in the pages ahead help you find a glimpse of both.

Ruskin Bond

THE ROOM ON THE ROOF
(An Excerpt)

The afternoon was warm and lazy, unusually so for spring; very quiet, as though resting in the interval between the spring and the coming summer. There was no sign of the missionary's wife or the sweeper boy when Rusty returned, but Mr Harrison's car stood in the driveway of the house.

At sight of the car, Rusty felt a little weak and frightened; he had not expected his guardian to return so soon and had, in fact, almost forgotten his existence. But now he forgot all about the chaat shop and Somi and Ranbir, and ran up the veranda steps in a panic.

Mr Harrison was at the top of the veranda steps, standing behind the potted palms.

The boy said, 'Oh, hullo, sir, you're back!' He knew of nothing else to say, but tried to make his little piece sound enthusiastic.

'Where have you been all day?' asked Mr Harrison, without looking once at the startled boy. 'Our neighbours haven't seen much of you lately.'

'I've been for a walk, sir.'

'You have been to the bazaar.'

The boy hesitated before making a denial; the man's eyes were on him now, and to lie Rusty would have had to lower his eyes—and this he could not do…

'Yes, sir, I went to the bazaar.'

'May I ask why?'

'Because I had nothing to do.'

'If you had nothing to do, you could have visited our neighbours. The bazaar is not the place for you. You know that.'

'But nothing happened to me…'

'That is not the point,' said Mr Harrison, and now his normally dry voice took on a faint shrill note of excitement, and he spoke rapidly. 'The point is, I have told you never to visit the bazaar. You belong here, to this house, this road, these people. Don't go where you don't belong.'

Rusty wanted to argue, longed to rebel, but fear of Mr Harrison held him back. He wanted to resist the man's authority, but he was conscious of the supple malacca cane in the glass cupboard.

'I'm sorry, sir…'

But his cowardice did him no good. The guardian went over to the glass cupboard, brought out the cane, flexed it in his hands. He said, 'It is not enough to say you are sorry, you must be made to feel sorry. Bend over the sofa.'

The boy bent over the sofa, clenched his teeth and dug his fingers into the cushions. The cane swished through the air, landing on his bottom with a slap, knocking the dust from his pants. Rusty felt no pain. But his guardian waited, allowing the cut to sink in, then he administered the second stroke, and this time it hurt, it stung into the boy's buttocks, burning up the flesh, conditioning it for the remaining cuts.

At the sixth stroke of the supple malacca cane, which was usually the last, Rusty let out a wild whoop, leapt over the sofa and charged from the room.

He lay groaning on his bed until the pain had eased.

But the flesh was so sore that he could not touch the place where the cane had fallen. Wriggling out of his pants, he examined his backside in the mirror. Mr Harrison had been most accurate: a thick purple welt stretched across both cheeks, and a little blood trickled down the boy's thigh. The blood had a cool, almost soothing effect, but the sight of it made Rusty feel faint.

He lay down and moaned for pleasure. He pitied himself enough to want to cry, but he knew the futility of tears. But the pain and the sense of injustice he felt were both real.

A shadow fell across the bed. Someone was at the window, and Rusty looked up.

The sweeper boy showed his teeth.

'What do you want?' asked Rusty gruffly.

'You hurt, chotta sahib?'

The sweeper boy's sympathies provoked only suspicion in Rusty.

'You told Mr Harrison where I went!' said Rusty.

But the sweeper boy cocked his head to one side, and asked innocently, 'Where you went, chotta sahib?'

'Oh, never mind. Go away.'

'But you hurt?'

'Get out!' shouted Rusty.

The smile vanished, leaving only a sad frightened look in the sweeper boy's eyes.

Rusty hated hurting people's feelings, but he was not accustomed to familiarity with servants; and yet, only a few minutes ago, he had been beaten for visiting the bazaar where there were so many like the sweeper boy.

The sweeper boy turned from the window, leaving wet fingermarks on the sill; then lifted his buckets from the ground and, with his knees bent to take the weight, walked away. His feet splashed a little in the water he had spilt, and the soft red mud flew up and flecked his legs.

Angry with his guardian and with the servant and most of all with himself, Rusty buried his head in his pillow and tried to shut out reality; he forced a dream, in which he was thrashing Mr Harrison until the guardian begged for mercy.

♦

In the early morning, when it was still dark, Ranbir stopped in the jungle behind Mr Harrison's house, and slapped his drum. His thick mass of hair was covered with red dust and his body, naked but for a cloth round his waist, was smeared green; he looked like a painted god, a green god. After a minute, he slapped the drum again, then sat down on his heels and waited.

Rusty woke to the sound of the second drum-beat, and lay in bed and listened; it was repeated, travelling over the still air and in through the bedroom window. *Dhum!*... A double-beat now, one deep, one high, insistent, questioning... Rusty remembered his promise, that he would play Holi with Ranbir, meet him in the jungle when he beat the drum. But he had made the promise on the condition that his guardian did not return; he could not possibly keep it now, not after the thrashing he had received.

Dhum-dhum, spoke the drum in the forest; dhum-dhum, impatient and getting annoyed...

'Why can't he shut up,' muttered Rusty, 'does he want to wake Mr Harrison…'

Holi, the festival of colours, the arrival of spring, the rebirth of the new year, the awakening of love, what were these things to him, they did not concern his life, he could not start a new life, not for one day…and besides, it all sounded very primitive, this throwing of colour and beating of drums…

Dhum-dhum!

The boy sat up in bed.

The sky had grown lighter.

From the distant bazaar came a new music, many drums and voices, faint but steady, growing in rhythm and excitement. The sound conveyed something to Rusty, something wild and emotional, something that belonged to his dream-world, and on a sudden impulse he sprang out of bed.

He went to the door and listened; the house was quiet, he bolted the door. The colours of Holi, he knew, would stain his clothes, so he did not remove his pyjamas. In an old pair of flattened rubber-soled tennis shoes, he climbed out of the window and ran over the dew-wet grass, down the path behind the house, over the hill and into the jungle.

When Ranbir saw the boy approach, he rose from the ground. The long hand-drum, the dholak, hung at his waist. As he rose, the sun rose. But the sun did not look as fiery as Ranbir who, in Rusty's eyes, appeared as a painted demon, rather than as a god.

'You are late, mister,' said Ranbir, 'I thought you were not coming.'

He had both his fists closed, but when he walked towards Rusty he opened them, smiling widely, a white smile in a green face. In his right hand was the red dust and in his left hand the green dust. And with his right hand, he rubbed the red dust on Rusty's left cheek, and then with the other hand, he put the green dust on the boy's right cheek; then he stood back and looked at Rusty and laughed. Then, according to the custom, he embraced the bewildered boy. It was a wrestler's hug, and Rusty winced breathlessly.

'Come,' said Ranbir, 'let us go and make the town a rainbow.'

◆

And truly, that day there was an outbreak of spring.

The sun came up, and the bazaar woke up. The walls of the houses were suddenly patched with splashes of colour, and just as suddenly the trees seemed to have burst into flower; for in the forest there were armies of rhododendrons, and by the river the poinsettias danced; the cherry and the plum were in blossom; the snow in the mountains had melted, and the streams were rushing torrents; the new leaves on the trees were full of sweetness, the young grass held both dew and sun, and made an emerald of every dewdrop.

The infection of spring spread simultaneously through the world of man and the world of nature, and made them one.

Ranbir and Rusty moved round the hill, keeping in the fringe of the jungle until they had skirted not only the European community but also the smart shopping centre. They came down dirty little side-streets where the walls of houses, stained with the wear and tear of many years of meagre habitation, were now stained again with the vivid colours of Holi. They came to the Clock Tower.

At the Clock Tower, spring had really been declared open. Clouds of coloured dust rose in the air and spread, and jets of water—green and orange and purple, all rich emotional colours—burst out everywhere.

Children formed groups. They were armed mainly with bicycle pumps, or pumps fashioned from bamboo stems, from which squirted liquid colour. The children paraded the main road, chanting shrilly and clapping their hands. The men and women preferred the dust to the water. They too sang, but their chanting held a significance, their hands and fingers drummed the rhythms of spring, the same rhythms, the same songs that belonged to this day every year of their lives.

Ranbir was met by some friends and greeted with great hilarity. A bicycle pump was directed at Rusty and a jet of sooty black water squirted into his face.

Blinded for a moment, Rusty blundered about in great confusion. A horde of children bore down on him, and he was subjected to a pumping from all sides. His shirt and pyjamas, drenched through, stuck to his skin; then someone gripped the end of his shirt and tugged at it until it tore and came away. Dust was thrown on the boy, on his face and body, roughly and with full force, and his tender, under-exposed skin smarted beneath the onslaught.

Then his eyes cleared. He blinked and looked wildly round at the group of boys and girls who cheered and danced in front of him. His body was running mostly with sooty black, streaked with red, and his mouth seemed full of it too, and he began to spit.

Then, one by one, Ranbir's friends approached Rusty.

Gently, they rubbed dust on the boy's cheeks, and embraced him; they were like so many flaming demons that Rusty could not distinguish one from the other. But this gentle greeting, coming so soon after the stormy bicycle-pump attack, bewildered Rusty even more.

Ranbir said, 'Now you are one of us, come,' and Rusty went with him and the others.

'Suri is hiding,' cried someone. 'He has locked himself in his house and won't play Holi!'

'Well, he will have to play,' said Ranbir, 'even if we break the house down.'

Suri, who dreaded Holi, had decided to spend the day in a state of siege; and had set up camp in his mother's kitchen, where there were provisions enough for the whole day. He listened to his playmates calling to him from the courtyard, and ignored their invitations, jeers and threats; the door was strong and well barricaded. He settled himself beneath a table, and turned the pages of the English nudists' journal, which he bought every month chiefly for its photographic value.

But the youths outside, intoxicated by the drumming and shouting and high spirits, were not going to be done out of the pleasure of discomfiting Suri. So they acquired a ladder and made their entry into the kitchen by the skylight.

Suri squealed with fright. The door was opened and he was bundled out, and his spectacles were trampled.

'My glasses!' he screamed. 'You've broken them!'

'You can afford a dozen pairs!' jeered one of his antagonists.

'But I can't see, you fools, I can't see!'

'He can't see!' cried someone in scorn. 'For once in his life, Suri can't see what's going on! Now, whenever he spies, we'll smash his glasses!'

Not knowing Suri very well, Rusty could not help pitying the frantic boy. 'Why don't you let him go?' he asked Ranbir. 'Don't force him if he doesn't want to play.'

'But this is the only chance we have of repaying him for all his dirty tricks. It is the only day on which no one is afraid of him!'

Rusty could not imagine how anyone could possibly be afraid of the pale, struggling, spindly-legged boy who was almost being torn apart, and was glad when the others had finished their sport with him.

All day Rusty roamed the town and countryside with Ranbir and his friends, and Suri was soon forgotten. For one day, Ranbir and his friends forgot their homes and their work and the problem of the next meal, and danced down the roads, out of the town and into the forest. And, for one day, Rusty forgot his guardian and the missionary's wife and the supple malacca cane, and ran with the others through the town and into the forest.

The crisp, sunny morning ripened into afternoon.

In the forest, in the cool dark silence of the jungle, they stopped singing and shouting, suddenly exhausted. They lay down in the shade of many trees, and the grass was soft and comfortable, and very soon everyone except Rusty was fast asleep.

Rusty was tired. He was hungry. He had lost his shirt and shoes, his feet were bruised, his body sore. It was only now, resting, that he noticed these things, for he had been caught up in the excitement of the colour game, overcome by an exhilaration he had never known. His fair hair was tousled and streaked with colour, and his eyes were wide with wonder.

He was exhausted now, but he was happy.

He wanted this to go on for ever, this day of feverish emotion, this life in another world. He did not want to leave the forest; it was safe, its earth soothed him, gathered him in so that the pain of his body became a pleasure...

He did not want to go home.

◆

Mr Harrison stood at the top of the veranda steps. The house was in darkness, but his cigarette glowed more brightly for it. A road lamp trapped the returning boy as he opened the gate, and Rusty knew he had been seen, but he didn't care much; if he had known that Mr Harrison had not recognized him, he would have turned back instead of walking resignedly up the garden path.

Mr Harrison did not move, nor did he appear to notice the boy's approach. It was only when Rusty climbed the veranda steps that his guardian moved and said, 'Who's that?'

Still he had not recognized the boy; and in that instant Rusty became aware of his own condition, for his body was a patchwork of paint. Wearing only torn pyjamas, he could, in the half-light, have easily been mistaken for the sweeper boy or someone else's servant. It must have been a newly acquired bazaar instinct that made the boy think of escape. He turned about.

But Mr Harrison shouted, 'Come here, you!' and the tone of his voice—the tone reserved for the sweeper boy—made Rusty stop.

'Come up here!' repeated Mr Harrison.

Rusty returned to the veranda, and his guardian switched on a light; but even now there was no recognition.

'Good evening, sir,' said Rusty.

Mr Harrison received a shock. He felt a wave of anger, and then a wave of pain: was this the boy he had trained and educated—this wild, ragged, ungrateful wretch, who did not know the difference between what was proper and what was improper, what was civilized and what was barbaric, what was decent and what was shameful—and had the years of training come to nothing? Mr Harrison came out of the shadows and cursed. He brought his hand down on the back of Rusty's neck, propelled him into the drawing-room, and pushed him across the room so violently that the boy lost his balance, collided with a table and rolled over on to the ground.

Rusty looked up from the floor to find his guardian standing over him, and in the man's right hand was the supple malacca cane and the cane was twitching.

Mr Harrison's face was twitching too, it was full of fire. His lips were stitched together, sealed up with the ginger moustache, and he looked at the boy with narrowed, unblinking eyes.

'Filth!' he said, almost spitting the words in the boy's face. 'My God, what filth!'

Rusty stared fascinated at the deep yellow nicotine stains on the fingers of his guardian's raised hand. Then the wrist moved suddenly and the cane cut across the boy's face like a knife, stabbing and burning into his cheek.

Rusty cried out and cowered back against the wall; he could feel the blood trickling across his mouth. He looked round desperately for a means of escape, but the man was in front of him, over him, and the wall was behind.

Mr Harrison broke into a torrent of words. 'How can you call yourself an Englishman, how can you come back to this house in such a condition? In what gutter, in what brothel have you been! Have you seen yourself? Do you know what you look like?'

'No,' said Rusty, and for the first time he did not address his guardian as 'sir'. 'I don't care what I look like.'

'You don't...well, I'll tell you what you look like! You look like the mongrel that you are!'

'That's a lie!' exclaimed Rusty.

'It's the truth. I've tried to bring you up as an Englishman, as your father would have wished. But, as you won't have it our way, I'm telling you that he was about the only thing English about you. You're no better than the sweeper boy!'

Rusty flared into a temper, showing some spirit for the first time in his life. 'I'm no better than the sweeper boy, but I am as good as him! I'm as good as you! I'm as good as anyone!' And, instead of cringing to take the cut from the cane, he flung himself at his guardian's legs. The cane swished through the air, grazing the boy's back. Rusty wrapped his arms round his guardian's legs and pulled on them with all his strength.

Mr Harrison went over, falling flat on his back.

The suddenness of the fall must have knocked the breath from his body, because for a moment he did not move.

Rusty sprang to his feet. The cut across his face had stung him to madness, to an unreasoning hate, and he did what previously he would only have dreamt of doing. Lifting a vase of the missionary's wife's best sweet peas off the glass cupboard, he flung it at his guardian's face. It hit him on the chest, but the water and flowers flopped out over his face. He tried to get up; but he was speechless.

The look of alarm on Mr Harrison's face gave Rusty greater courage. Before the man could recover his feet and his balance, Rusty gripped him by the collar and pushed him backwards, until they both fell over on to the floor. With one hand still twisting the collar; the boy slapped his guardian's face. Mad with the pain in his own face, Rusty hit the man again and again, wildly and awkwardly, but with the giddy thrill of knowing he could do it: he was a child no longer, he was nearly seventeen, he was a man. He could inflict pain, that was a wonderful discovery; there was a power in his body—a devil or a god—and he gained confidence in his power; and he was a man!

'Stop that, stop it!' The shout of a hysterical woman brought

Rusty to his senses. He still held his guardian by the throat, but he stopped hitting him. Mr Harrison's face was very red. The missionary's wife stood in the doorway, her face white with fear. She was under the impression that Mr Harrison was being attacked by a servant or some bazaar hooligan. Rusty did not wait until she found her tongue but, with a new-found speed and agility, darted out of the drawing-room.

He made his escape from the bedroom window. From the gate he could see the missionary's wife silhouetted against the drawing-room light. He laughed out loud. The woman swivelled round and came forward a few steps. And Rusty laughed again and began running down the road to the bazaar.

♦

It was late. The smart shops and restaurants were closed. In the bazaar, oil lamps hung outside each doorway; people were asleep on the steps and platforms of shopfronts, some huddled in blankets, others rolled tight into themselves. The road, which during the day was a busy, noisy crush of people and animals, was quiet and deserted. Only a lean dog still sniffed in the gutter. A woman sang in a room high above the street—a plaintive, tremulous song—and in the far distance a jackal cried to the moon. But the empty, lifeless street was very deceptive; if the roofs could have been removed from but a handful of buildings, it would be seen that life had not really stopped but, beautiful and ugly, persisted through the night.

It was past midnight, though the Clock Tower had no way of saying it. Rusty was in the empty street, and the chaat shop was closed, a sheet of tarpaulin draped across the front. He looked up and down the road, hoping to meet someone he knew; the chaat-walla, he felt sure, would give him a blanket for the night and a place to sleep; and the next day when Somi came to meet him, he would tell his friend of his predicament, that he had run away from his guardian's house and did not intend returning. But he would have to wait till morning: the chaat shop was shuttered, barred and bolted.

He sat down on the steps; but the stone was cold and his thin cotton pyjamas offered no protection. He folded his arms and huddled up in a corner, but still he shivered. His feet were becoming numb, lifeless.

Rusty had not fully realized the hazards of the situation. He was still mad with anger and rebellion and, though the blood on his cheek had dried, his face was still smarting. He could not think clearly: the present was confusing and unreal and he could not see beyond it; what worried him was the cold and the discomfort and the pain.

The singing stopped in the high window. Rusty looked up and saw a beckoning hand. As no one else in the street showed any signs of life, Rusty got up and walked across the road until he was under the window. The woman pointed to a stairway, and he mounted it, glad of the hospitality he was being offered.

The stairway seemed to go to the stars, but it turned suddenly to lead into the woman's room. The door was slightly ajar; he knocked and a voice said, 'Come...'

The room was filled with perfume and burning incense. A musical instrument lay in one corner. The woman reclined on a bed, her hair scattered about the pillow; she had a round, pretty face, but she was losing her youth, and the fat showed in rolls at her exposed waist. She smiled at the boy, and beckoned again.

'Thank you,' said Rusty, closing the door. 'Can I sleep here?'

'Where else?' said the woman.

'Just for tonight.'

She smiled, and waited. Rusty stood in front of her, his hands behind his back.

'Sit down,' she said, and patted the bedclothes beside her.

Reverently, and as respectfully as he could, Rusty sat down.

The woman ran little fair fingers over his body, and drew his head to hers; their lips were very close, almost touching, and their breathing sounded terribly loud to Rusty, but he only said, 'I am hungry.'

A poet, thought the woman, and kissed him full on the lips; but the boy drew away in embarrassment, unsure of himself, liking the woman on the bed and yet afraid of her...

'What is wrong?' she asked. 'I'm tired,' he said. The woman's friendly smile turned to a look of scorn; but she saw that he was only a boy whose eyes were full of unhappiness, and she could not help pitying him.

'You can sleep here,' she said, 'until you have lost your tiredness.'

But he shook his head. 'I will come some other time,' he said, not wishing to hurt the woman's feelings. They were both pitying each other, liking each other, but not enough to make them understand each other.

Rusty left the room. Mechanically, he descended the staircase, and walked up the bazaar road, past the silent sleeping forms, until he reached the Clock Tower. To the right of the Clock Tower was a broad stretch of grassland where, during the day, cattle grazed and children played and young men like Ranbir wrestled and kicked footballs. But now, at night, it was a vast empty space.

But the grass was soft, like the grass in the forest, and Rusty walked the length of the maidan. He found a bench and sat down, warmer for the walk. A light breeze was blowing across the maidan, pleasant and refreshing, playing with his hair. Around him everything was dark and silent and lonely. He had got away from the bazaar, which held the misery of beggars and homeless children and starving dogs, and could now concentrate on his own misery; for there was nothing like loneliness for making Rusty conscious of his unhappy state. Madness and freedom and violence were new to him: loneliness was familiar, something he understood.

Rusty was alone. Until tomorrow, he was alone for the rest of his life.

If tomorrow there was no Somi at the chaat shop, no Ranbir, then what would he do? This question badgered him persistently, making him an unwilling slave to reality. He did not know where his friends lived, he had no money, he could not ask the chaat-walla for credit on the strength of two visits. Perhaps he should return to the amorous lady in the bazaar; perhaps… but no, one thing was certain, he would never return to his guardian…

The moon had been hidden by clouds, and presently there was a drizzle. Rusty did not mind the rain, it refreshed him and made the colour run from his body; but, when it began to fall harder, he started shivering again. He felt sick. He got up, rolled his ragged pyjamas up to the thighs and crawled under the bench.

There was a hollow under the bench, and at first Rusty found it quite comfortable. But there was no grass and gradually the earth began to soften: soon he was on his hands and knees in a pool of muddy water, with the slush oozing up through his fingers and toes. Crouching there, wet and cold and muddy, he was overcome by a feeling of helplessness and self-pity: everyone and everything seemed to have turned against him; not only his people but also the bazaar and the chaat shop and even the elements. He admitted to himself that he had been too impulsive in rebelling and running away from home; perhaps there was still time to return and beg for Mr Harrison's forgiveness. But could his behaviour be forgiven? Might he not be clapped into irons for attempted murder? Most certainly he would be given another beating: not six strokes this time but nine.

His only hope was Somi. If not Somi, then Ranbir. If not Ranbir…well, it was no use thinking further, there was no one else to think of.

The rain had ceased. Rusty crawled out from under the bench, and stretched his cramped limbs. The moon came out from a cloud and played with his wet, glistening body, and showed him the vast, naked loneliness of the maidan and his own insignificance. He longed now for the presence of people, be they beggars or women, and he broke into a trot, and the trot became a run, a frightened run, and he did not stop until he reached the Clock Tower.

ONCE YOU HAVE LIVED
WITH MOUNTAINS

It was while I was living in England in the jostle and drizzle of London, that I remembered the Himalayas at their most vivid. I had grown up amongst those great blue and brown mountains, they had nourished my blood, and though I was separated from them by thousands of miles of ocean, plain and desert, I could not forget them. It is always the same with mountains. Once you have lived with them for any length of time, you belong to them. There is no escape.

And so, in London in March, the fog became a mountain mist and the boom of traffic became the boom of the Ganges emerging from the foothills. I remembered a little mountain path which led my restless feet into a cool sweet forest of oak and rhododendron and then on to the windswept crest of a naked hilltop. The hill was called Cloud's End. It commanded a view of the plains on one side, and of the snow peaks on the other. Little silver rivers twisted across the valley below, where the rice fields formed a patchwork of emerald green. And on the hill itself the wind made a 'hoo-hoo-hoo' in the branches of the tall deodars where it found itself trapped. During the rains, clouds enveloped the valley but left the hills alone, an island in the sky. Wild sorrel grew among the rocks, and there were many flowers—convolvulus, clover, wild begonia, dandelion—sprinkling the hillside.

On a spur of the hill stood the ruins of an old building, the roof of which had long since disappeared and the rain had beaten the stone floors smooth and yellow. Moss, ferns and Maidenhair grew from the walls. In a hollow beneath a flight of worn stone steps a wild cat had made its home. It was a beautiful grey creature, black-striped with pale great eyes. Sometimes it watched me from the steps or the wall, but it never came near.

No one lived on the hill, except occasionally a coal-burner in a temporary grass thatched hut. But villagers used the path for grazing their sheep and cattle on the grassy slopes. Each cow or sheep had a bell suspended from its neck to let the shepherd boy know its whereabouts.

The boy could then lie in the sun and eat wild strawberries without fear of losing his animals. I remembered some of the shepherd boys and girls. There was a boy who played the flute. Its rough, sweet, straightforward notes travelled clearly through the mountain air. He would greet me with a nod of his head, without taking the flute from his lips.

There was a girl who was nearly always cutting grass for fodder. She wore heavy bangles on her feet and long silver earrings. She did not speak much either, but she always had a wide smile on her face when she met me on the path. She used to sing to herself, or to the sheep, or to the grass, or to the sickle in her hand. And there was a boy who carried milk into town (a distance of about five miles) who would often fall into step with me to hold a long conversation. He had never been away from the hills or in a large city. He had never been on a train.

I told him about the cities and he told me about his village, how they made bread from maize, how fish were to be caught in the mountain streams, how the bears came to steal his father's pumpkins. Whenever the pumpkins were ripe, he told me, the bears would come and carry them off. These things I remembered—these, and the smell of pine needles, the silver of oak leaves and the red of maple, the call of the Himalayan cuckoo, and the mist, like a wet face-cloth, pressing against the hills.

Odd, how some little incident, some snatch of conversation comes back to one again and again in the most unlikely places. Standing in the aisle of a crowded tube train on a Monday morning, my nose tucked into the back page of someone else's newspaper, I suddenly had a vision of a bear making off with a ripe pumpkin! A bear and a pumpkin—and there, between Belsize Park and the Tottenham Court Road station, all the smells and sounds of the Himalayas came rushing back to me.

THE POSTMAN KNOCKS

As a freelance writer, most of my adult life has revolved around the coming of the postman. 'A cheque in the mail,' is something that every struggling writer looks forward to. It might, of course, arrive by courier, or it might not come at all. But for the most part, the acceptances and rejections of my writing life, along with editorial correspondence, readers' letters, page proofs and author's copies—how welcome they are!—come through the post.

The postman has always played a very real and important part in my life, and continues to do so. He climbs my twenty-one steps every afternoon, knocks loudly on my door—three raps, so that I know it's him and not some inquisitive tourist—and gives me my registered mail or speed-post with a smile and a bit of local gossip. The gossip is important. I like to know what's happening in the bazaar—who's getting married, who's standing for election, who ran away with the headmaster's wife, and whose funeral procession is passing by. He deserves a bonus for this sort of information.

The courier boy, by contrast, shouts to me from the road below and I have to go down to him. He's mortally afraid of dogs and there are three in the building. My postman isn't bothered by dogs. He comes in all weathers, and he comes on foot except when someone gives him a lift. He turns up when it's snowing, or when it's raining cats and dogs, or when there's a heat wave, and he's quite philosophical about it all. He meets all kinds of people. He has seen joy and sorrow in the homes he visits. He knows something about life. If he wasn't a philosopher to begin with, he will certainly be one by the time he retires.

Of course, not all postmen are paragons of virtue. A few years ago, we had a postman who never got further than the country liquor shop in the bazaar. The mail would pile up there for days, until he sobered up and condescended to deliver it. In due course, he was banished to another route, where there were no liquor shops.

We take the postman for granted today, but there was a time, over a hundred years ago, when the carrying of the mails was a hazardous venture, and the mail-runner, or *hirkara* as he was called, had to be armed with sword or spear. Letters were carried in leather wallets on the backs of runners, who were changed at stages of eight miles. At night, the runners were accompanied by torch-bearers—in wilder parts, by drummers called *dug-dugi wallas*—to frighten away wild animals.

The tiger population was considerable at the time, and tigers were a real threat to travellers or anyone who ventured far from their town or village. Mail-runners often fell victim to man-eating tigers. The mail-runners (most of them tribals) were armed with bows and arrows, but these were seldom effective.

In the Hazaribagh district (through which the mail had to be carried, on its way from Calcutta to Allahabad) there appears to have been a concentration of man-eating tigers. There were four passes through this district, and the tigers had them well covered. Williamson, writing in 1810, tells us that the passes were so infested with tigers that the roads were almost impassable. 'Day after day, for nearly a fortnight, some of the dak people were carried off at one or other of these passes.'

In spite of these hazards, a letter sent by dak runner used to take twelve days to reach Meerut from Calcutta. It takes about the same time today, unless you use speed-post.

At up country stations, the collector of Land Revenue was the Postmaster. He was given a small postal establishment, consisting of a *munshi*, a *matsaddi* or sorter, and thirty or for, runners whose pay, in 1804, was five rupees a month. The maintenance of the dak cost the government (i.e., the East India Company) twenty-five rupees a month for each stage of eight miles. Postage stamps were introduced in 1854.

My father was an enthusiastic philatelist, and when I was a small boy I could sit and watch him pore over his stamp collection, which included several early and valuable Indian issues. He would grumble at the very dark and smudgy postmarks which obliterated most of Queen Victoria's profile from the stamps. This was due to the composition of the ink used for cancelling the earlier stamps. It was composed of two parts lamp-black, four parts linseed oil and three and a half of vinegar.

Letter-distributing peons, or postmen, were always smartly turned out: 'A red turban, a light green chapkan, a small leather belt over the breast and right shoulder, with a chaprass attached showing the peon's number and having the words "Post Office Peon" in English and in two vernaculars, and a bell suspended by a leather strap from the left shoulder.'

Today's postmen are more casual in their attire, although I believe they are still entitled to uniforms. The general public doesn't care how they are dressed, as long as they turn up with those letters containing rakhis or money orders from soldiers, peons and husbands. This is where the postman still scores over the fax and email.

To return to our mail-runners, they were eventually replaced by the *dak-ghari*, the equivalent of the English 'coach and pair'—which gradually established itself throughout the country.

A survivor into the 1940s, my great-aunt Lillian recalled that in the late nineteenth century, before the coming of the railway, the only way of getting to Dehradun was by the dak-ghari or Night Mail. Dak-ghari ponies were difficult animals, she told me—'always attempting to turn around and get into the carriage with the passengers!' But once they started there was no stopping them. It was a gallop all the way to the first stage, where the ponies were changed to the accompaniment of a bugle blown by the coachman, in true Dickensian fashion.

The journey through the Siwaliks really began—as it still does—through the Mohand Pass. The ascent starts with a gradual gradient which increases as the road becomes more steep and winding. At this stage of the journey, drums were beaten (if it was day) and torches lit (if it was night) because sometimes wild elephants resented the approach of the dak-ghari and, trumpeting a challenge, would throw the ponies into confusion and panic, and send them racing back to the plains.

After 1900, great-aunt Lillian used the train. But the main bus from Saharanpur to Mussoorie still uses the old route through the Siwaliks. And if you are lucky, you may see a herd of wild elephants crossing the road on its way to the Ganga.

And even today, in remote parts of the country, in isolated hill areas where there are no motorable roads, the mail is carried on foot, the postman often covering five or six miles every day. He never runs, true, and he might sometimes stop for a glass of tea and a game of cards en-route, but he is a reminder of those early pioneers of the postal system, the mail-runners of India.

◆

Let me not cavil at my unexpected visitors. Sometimes they turn out to be very nice people—like the gentleman from Pune who brought me a bottle of whisky and then sat down and drank most of it himself.

WHITE CLOUDS, GREEN MOUNTAINS

Towards the end of September, those few monsoon clouds that still linger over the Himalayas are no longer burdened with rain and are able to assume unusual shapes and patterns, chasing each other across the sky and disappearing in spectacular sunset formations.

I have always found this to be the best time of the year in the hills. The sun-drenched hillsides are still an emerald green; the air is crisp, but winter's bite is still a month or two away; and for those who still like to take to the open road on foot, there are springs, streams and waterfalls tumbling over rocks that remain dry for most of the year. The lizard that basked on a sun-baked slab of granite last May is missing, but in his place the spotted forktail trips daintily among the boulders in a stream; and the strident sound of the cicadas is gradually replaced by the gentler trilling of the crickets and grasshoppers.

Cicadas, as you probably know, make their music with their legs, which are moved like the bows of violins against their bodies. It's rather like an orchestra tuning up but never quite getting on with the overture or symphony. Aunt Ruby, who is a little deaf, can nevertheless hear the cicadas when they are at their loudest. She lives not far from a large boarding-school, and one day when I remarked that I could hear the school choir or choral group singing, she nodded and remarked: 'Yes, dear. They do it with their legs, don't they?'

Come to think of it, that school choir does sound a bit squeaky.

Now, more than at any other time of the year, the wildflowers come into their own.

The hillside is covered with a sward of flowers and ferns. Sprays of wild ginger, tangles of clematis, flat clusters of yarrow and lady's mantle. The datura grows everywhere with its graceful white balls and prickly fruits. And the wild woodbine provides the stems from which the village boys make their flutes.

Aroids are plentiful and attract attention by their resemblance to snakes with protruding tongues—hence the popular name, cobra lily. This serpent's tongue is a perfect landing-stage for flies etc., who, crawling over the male flowers in their eager search for the liquor that lies at the base of the spike (a liquor that is most appealing to their depraved appetites), succeed in fertilizing the female flowers as they proceed. We see that it is not only humans who become addicted to alcohol. Bears have been known to get drunk on the juice of rhododendron flowers, while bumble bees can be out-and-out dipsomaniacs.

One of the more spectacular cobra lilies, which rejoices in the name *Sauromotum Guttatum*—ask your nearest botanist what that means!—bears a solitary leaf and purple spathe. When the seeds form, it withdraws the spike underground; and when the rains are over and the soil is not too damp, it sends it up again covered with scarlet berries. In the opinion of the hill folk, the appearance of the red spike is more to be relied on as a forecast of the end of the monsoon than any meteorological expertise. Up here on the ranges that fall between the Jumna and the Bhagirathi (known as the Rawain), we can be perfectly sure of fine weather a fortnight after the fiery spike appears.

But it is the commelina, more than any other Himalayan flower, that takes my breath away. The secret is in its colour—a pure pristine blue that seems to reflect the deepest blue of the sky. Towards the end of the rains it appears as if from nowhere, graces the hillside for the space of about two weeks, and disappears again until the following monsoon.

When I see the first commelina, I stand dumb before it and the world stands still while I worship. So absorbed do I become in its delicate beauty that I begin to doubt the reality of everything else in the world.

But only for a moment. The blare of a truck's horn reminds me that I am still lingering on the main road leading out of the hill station. A cloud of dust and blasts of diesel fumes are further indications that reality takes many different forms, assailing all my senses at once! Even my commelina seems to shrink from the onslaught. But as it is still there, I take heart and leave the highway for a lesser road.

Soon I have left the clutter of the town behind. What did Aunt Ruby say the other day? 'Stand still for five minutes, and they will build a hotel on top of you.'

Wasn't it Lot's wife who was turned into a pillar of salt when she looked back at the doomed city that had been her home? I have an uneasy feeling that I will be turned into a pillar of cement if I look back, so I plod on along the road to Devsari, a kindly village in the valley. It will be some time before 'developers' and big money boys get here, for no one will go to live where there is no driveway!

A tea shop beckons. How would one manage in the hills without these wayside tea shops? Miniature inns, they provide food, shelter and even lodging to dozens at a time.

I tackle some buns that have a pre-Independence look about them. They are rock-hard, to match the environment, but I manage to swallow some of the jagged pieces with the hot sweet tea, which is good.

MY TREES IN THE HIMALAYAS

Living in a cottage at seven thousand feet in the Garhwal Himalayas, I am fortunate to have a big window that opens out on the forest so that the trees are almost within my reach. If I jumped, I could land quite neatly in the arms of an oak or horse chestnut. I have never made that leap, but the big langurs—silver-grey monkeys with long, swishing tails—often spring from the trees onto my corrugated tin roof, making enough noise to frighten all the birds away.

Standing on its own outside my window is a walnut tree, and truly this is a tree for all seasons. In winter, the branches were bare; but they were smooth, straight and round like the arms of an apsara. In spring each limb produces a bright green spear of new growth, and by midsummer the entire tree is in leaf. Toward the end of the monsoon, the walnuts, encased in their green jackets, have reached maturity. When the jackets begin to split, you can see the hard brown shells of the nuts, and inside each shell is the delicious meat itself. Look closely at the nut, and you will notice that it is shaped rather like the human brain. No wonder the ancients prescribed walnuts for headaches.

Every year this tree gives me a basket of walnuts. But last year, the nuts were disappearing one by one, and I was at a loss as to who had been taking them. Could it have been Bijju, the milkman's small son? He was an inveterate tree climber, but he was usually to be found on the oak trees, gathering fodder for his herd. He admitted that his cows had enjoyed my dahlias, which they had eaten the previous week, but he stoutly denied having fed them walnuts, saying they did not care for them.

Later, I found a fat langur sitting in the walnut tree. I watched him for some time to see if he was going to help himself to the nuts, but he was only sunning himself. When he thought I wasn't looking, he came down and ate the geraniums; but he did not take any walnuts.

It wasn't the woodpecker either. He was out there every day, knocking furiously against the bark of the tree, trying to pry an insect out of a narrow crack. He was strictly non-vegetarian and none the worse for it.

The nuts seemed to disappear early in the morning while I was still in bed, so one day I surprised everyone, including myself by getting up before sunrise. I was just in time to catch the culprit climbing out of the walnut tree. She was an old woman who sometimes came to cut grass on the hillside. Her face was as wrinkled as the walnuts she had been pinching. But in spite of her age, her arms and legs were sturdy. When she saw me, she was as swift as a civet cat in getting out of the tree.

'And how many walnuts did you gather today, Grandmother?' I asked.

'Just two,' she said with a giggle, offering them to me on her open palm. I accepted one, and thus encouraged, she climbed higher into the tree and helped herself to the remaining nuts. It was impossible for me to object. I was taken with admiration for her agility. She must have been twice my age, but I knew I could never get up that tree. To the victor, the spoils!

Last winter, the PWD decided to take a new road past my doorstep, and the first casualty was the walnut tree. Along with a large number of different trees growing below the cottage, it fell to the contractors' axes.

Recently when I met the old woman on the road, I asked her, 'Where do you get your walnuts now, Grandmother?'

'Nowhere,' she answered stoically. 'That was the last walnut tree on the hillside.'

Unlike the prized walnuts, the horse chestnuts are inedible. Even the rhesus monkeys throw them away in disgust. But the tree itself is a friendly one, especially in summer when it is in full leaf. The lightest breeze makes the leaves break into conversation, and their rustle is a cheerful sound. The spring flowers of the horse chestnut look like candelabra, and when the blossoms fall, they carpet the hillside with their pale pink petals. It stands erect and dignified and does not bend with the wind. In spring, the new leaves, or needles, are a tender green, while during the monsoon, the tiny young cones spread like blossoms in the dark green folds of the branches.

The deodar enjoys the company of its own kind: where one deodar grows, there will be others. A walk in a deodar forest is awe-inspiring—surrounded on all sides by these great sentinels of the mountains, you feel as though the trees themselves are on the march.

I walk among the trees outside my window often, acknowledging their presence with a touch of my hand against their trunks. The oak has been there the longest, and the wind has bent its upper branches and twisted a few so that it looks shaggy and undistinguished. But it is a good tree for the privacy of birds. Sometimes it seems completely uninhabited until there is a whining sound, as of a helicopter approaching, and a party of long-tailed blue magpies flies across the forest glade.

Most of the pines near my home are on the next hillside. But there is a small Himalayan blue a little way below the cottage, and sometimes I sit beneath it to listen to the wind playing softly in its branches.

When I open the window at night, there is almost always something to listen to—the mellow whistle of a pygmy owlet, or the sharp cry of a barking deer. Sometimes, if I am lucky, I will see the moon coming up over the next mountain, and two distant deodars in perfect silhouette.

Some nights, sounds outside my window remain strange and mysterious. Perhaps they are the sounds of the trees themselves, stretching their limbs in the dark, shifting a little, flexing their fingers, whispering to one another. These great trees of the mountains, I feel they know me well, as I watch them and listen to their secrets, happy to rest my head beneath their outstretched arms.

DUST ON THE MOUNTAIN

I

Winter came and went, without so much as a drizzle. The hillside was brown all summer and the fields were bare. The old plough that was dragged over the hard ground by Bisnu's lean oxen made hardly any impression. Still, Bisnu kept his seeds ready for sowing. A good monsoon, and there would be plenty of maize and rice to see the family through the next winter.

Summer went its scorching way, and a few clouds gathered on the south-western horizon.

'The monsoon is coming,' announced Bisnu.

His sister Puja was at the small stream, washing clothes. 'If it doesn't come soon, the stream will dry up,' she said. 'See, it's only a trickle this year. Remember when there were so many different flowers growing here on the banks of the stream? This year there isn't one.'

'The winter was dry. It did not even snow,' said Bisnu.

'I cannot remember another winter when there was no snow,' said his mother. 'The year your father died, there was so much snow the villagers could not light his funeral pyre for hours.

And now there are fires everywhere.' She pointed to the next mountain, half-hidden by the smoke from a forest fire. At night they sat outside their small house, watching the fire spread. A red line stretched right across the mountain. Thousands of Himalayan trees were perishing in the flames. Oaks, deodars, maples, pines; trees that had taken hundreds of years to grow. And now a fire started carelessly by some campers had been carried up the mountain with the help of the dry grass and strong breeze.

There was no one to put it out. It would take days to die down by itself.

'If the monsoon arrives tomorrow, the fire will go out,' said Bisnu, ever the optimist. He was only twelve, but he was the man in the house; he had to see that there was enough food for the family and for the oxen, for the big black dog and the hens.

There were clouds the next day but they brought only a drizzle. 'It's just the beginning,' said Bisnu, as he placed a bucket of muddy water on the steps.

'It usually starts with a heavy downpour,' said his mother. But there were to be no downpours that year. Clouds gathered on the horizon but they were white and puffy and soon disappeared.

True monsoon clouds would have been dark and heavy with moisture. There were other signs—or lack of them—that warned of a long, dry summer. The birds were silent, or simply absent. The Himalayan barbet, who usually heralded the approach of the monsoon with strident calls from the top of a spruce tree, hadn't been seen or heard. And the cicadas, who played a deafening overture in the oaks at the first hint of rain, seemed to be missing altogether.

Puja's apricot tree usually gave them a basket full of fruit every summer. This year it produced barely a handful of apricots, lacking juice and flavour. The tree looked ready to die, its leaves curled up in despair. Fortunately, there was a store of walnuts, and a bin full of wheat grain and another of rice stored from the previous year, so they would not be entirely without food; but it looked as though there would be no fresh fruit or vegetables. And there would be nothing to store away for the following winter.

Money would be needed to buy supplies in Tehri, some thirty miles distant. And there was no money to be earned in the village.

'I will go to Mussoorie and find work,' announced Bisnu.

'But Mussoorie is a two-day journey by bus,' said his mother. 'There is no one there who can help you. And you may not get any work.'

'In Mussoorie there is plenty of work during the summer. Rich people come up from the plains for their holidays. It is full of hotels and shops and places where they can spend their money.'

'But they won't spend any money on you.'

'There is money to be made there. And if not, I will come home. I can walk back over the Nag Tibba mountain. It will take only two-and-a-half days and I will save the bus fare!'

'Don't go, Bhai,' pleaded Puja.

'There will be no one to prepare your food—you will only get sick.'

But Bisnu had made up his mind so he put a few belongings in a cloth shoulder bag, while his mother prised several rupee coins out of a cache in the wall of their living room. Puja prepared a special breakfast of parathas and an egg scrambled with onions, the hen having laid just one for the occasion. Bisnu put some of the parathas in his bag. Then, waving goodbye to his mother and sister, he set off down the road from the village. After walking for a mile, he reached the highway where there was a hamlet with a bus stop. A number of villagers were waiting patiently for a bus. It was an hour late but they were used to that. As long as it arrived safely and got them to their destination, they would be content. They were patient people. And although Bisnu wasn't quite so patient, he too had learnt how to wait—for late buses and late monsoons.

II

Along the valley and over the mountains went the little bus with its load of frail humans. A little misjudgement on the part of the driver, and they would all be dashed to pieces on the rocks far below.

'How tiny we are,' thought Bisnu, looking up at the towering peaks and the immensity of the sky. 'Each of us no more than a raindrop... And I wish we had a few raindrops!'

There were still fires burning to the north but the road went south, where there were no forests anyway, just bare brown hillsides. Down near the river there were small paddy fields but unfortunately rivers ran downhill and not uphill, and there was no inexpensive way in which the water could be brought up the steep slopes to the fields that depended on rainfall.

Bisnu stared out of the bus window at the river running far below. On either bank huge boulders lay exposed, for the level of the water had fallen considerably during the past few months. 'Why are there no trees here?' he asked aloud, and received the attention of a fellow passenger, an old man in the next seat who had been keeping up a relentless dry coughing. Even though it was a warm day, he wore a woollen cap and had an old muffler wrapped about his neck.

'There were trees here once,' he said. 'But the contractors took the deodars for furniture and houses. And the pines were tapped to death for resin. And the oaks were stripped of their leaves to feed the cattle—you can still see a few tree skeletons if you look hard—and the bushes that remained were finished off by the goats!'

'When did all this happen?' asked Bisnu.

'A few years ago. And it's still happening in other areas, although it's forbidden now to cut trees. The only forests that remain are in remote places where there are no roads.' A fit of coughing came over him, but he had found a good listener and was eager to continue. 'The road helps you and me to get about but it also makes it easier for others to do mischief. Rich men from the cities come here and buy up what they want—land, trees, people!'

'What takes you to Mussoorie, Uncle?' asked Bisnu politely. He always addressed elderly people as uncle or aunt.

'I have a cough that won't go away. Perhaps they can do something for it at the hospital in Mussoorie. Doctors don't like coming to villages, you know—there's no money to be made in villages. So we must go to the doctors in the towns. I had a brother who could not be cured in Mussoorie. They told him to go to Delhi. He sold his buffaloes and went to Delhi, but there they told him it was too late to do anything. He died on the way back. I won't go to Delhi. I don't wish to die amongst strangers.'

'You'll get well, Uncle,' said Bisnu.

'Bless you for saying so. And you—what takes you to the big town?'

'Looking for work—we need money at home.'

'It is always the same. There are many like you who must

go out in search of work. But don't be led astray. Don't let your friends persuade you to go to Bombay to become a film star! It is better to be hungry in your village than to be hungry on the streets of Bombay. I had a nephew who went to Bombay. The smugglers put him to work selling *afeem* (opium) and now he is in jail. Keep away from the big cities, boy. Earn your money and go home.'

'I'll do that, Uncle. My mother and sister will expect me to return before the summer season is over.'

The old man nodded vigorously and began coughing again. Presently he dozed off. The interior of the bus smelt of tobacco smoke and petrol fumes and as a result Bisnu had a headache. He kept his face near the open window to get as much fresh air as possible, but the dust kept getting into his mouth and eyes.

Several dusty hours later the bus got into Mussoorie, honking its horn furiously at everything in sight. The passengers, looking dazed, got down and went their different ways. The old man trudged off to the hospital.

Bisnu had to start looking for a job straightaway. He needed a lodging for the night and he could not afford even the cheapest of hotels. So he went from one shop to another, and to all the little restaurants and eating places, asking for work—anything in exchange for a bed, a meal and a minimum wage. A boy at one of the sweet shops told him there was a job at the Picture Palace, one of the town's three cinemas. The hill station's main road was crowded with people, for the season was just starting. Most of them were tourists who had come up from Delhi and other large towns.

The street lights had come on, and the shops were lighting up, when Bisnu presented himself at the Picture Palace.

III

The man who ran the cinema's tea stall had just sacked the previous helper for his general clumsiness. Whenever he engaged a new boy (which was fairly often) he started him off with the warning: 'I will be keeping a record of all the cups and plates you break, and their cost will be deducted from your salary at the end of the month.'

As Bisnu's salary had been fixed at fifty rupees a month, he would have to be very careful if he were going to receive any of it.

'In my first month,' said Chittru, one of the three tea stall boys, 'I broke six cups and five saucers, and my pay came to three rupees! Better be careful!'

Bisnu's job was to help prepare the tea and samosas, serve these refreshments to the public during intervals in the film, and later wash up the dishes. In addition to his salary, he was allowed to drink as much tea as he wanted or could hold in his stomach. But the sugar supply was kept to a minimum.

Bisnu went to work immediately and it was not long before he was as well-versed in his duties as the other two tea boys, Chittru and Bali. Chittru was an easy-going, lazy boy who always tried to place the brunt of his work on someone else's shoulders. But he was generous and lent Bisnu five rupees during the first week. Bali, besides being a tea boy, had the enviable job of being the poster boy. As the cinema was closed during the mornings, Bali would be busy either pushing the big poster board around Mussoorie, or sticking posters on convenient walls.

'Posters are very useful,' he claimed. 'They prevent old walls from falling down.'

Chittru had relatives in Mussoorie and slept at their house.

But both Bisnu and Bali were on their own and had to sleep at the cinema. After the last show, the hall was locked up, so they could not settle down in the expensive seats as they would have liked! They had to sleep on a dirty mattress in the foyer, near the ticket office, where they were often at the mercy of icy Himalayan winds.

Bali made things more comfortable by setting his poster board at an angle to the wall, which gave them a little alcove where they could sleep protected from the wind. As they had only one blanket each, they placed their blankets together and rolled themselves into a tight warm ball.

During shows, when Bisnu took the tea around, there was nearly always someone who would be rude and offensive. Once when he spilt some tea on a college student's shoes, he received a hard kick on the shin. He complained to the tea stall owner, but his employer said, 'The customer is always right. You should have got out of the way in time!'

As he began to get used to this life, Bisnu found himself taking an interest in some of the regular customers.

There was, for instance, the large gentleman with the soup-strainer moustache, who drank his tea from the saucer. As he drank, his lips worked like a suction pump, and the tea, after a brief agitation in the saucer, would disappear in a matter of seconds. Bisnu often wondered if there was something lurking in the forests of that gentleman's upper lip, something that would suddenly spring out and fall upon him! The boys took great pleasure in exchanging anecdotes about the peculiarities of some of the customers.

Bisnu had never seen such bright, painted women before. The girls in his village, including his sister Puja, were good-looking and often sturdy; but they did not use perfumes or make-up like these more prosperous women from the towns of the plains. Wearing expensive clothes and jewellery, they never gave Bisnu more than a brief, bored glance. Other women were more inclined to notice him, favouring him with kind words and a small tip when he took away the cups and plates. He found he could make a few rupees a month in tips; and when he received his first month's pay, he was able to send some of it home.

Chittru accompanied him to the post office and helped him to fill in the money order form. Bisnu had been to the village school, but be wasn't used to forms and official paperwork. As Chittru had been in the town for a while, he knew all about them, even though he could just about read and write.

Walking back to the cinema, Chittru said, 'We can make more money at the limestone quarries.'

'All right, let's try them,' said Bisnu.

'Not now,' said Chittru, who enjoyed the busy season in the hill station. 'After the season—after the monsoon.'

But there was still no monsoon to speak of, just an occasional drizzle which did little to clear the air of the dust that blew up from the plains. Bisnu wondered how his mother and sister were faring at home. A wave of homesickness swept over him. The hill station, with all its glitter, was just a pretty gift box with nothing inside.

One day in the cinema Bisnu saw the old man who had been with him on the bus. He greeted him like a long lost friend. At first the old man did not recognize the boy, but when Bisnu asked him if he had recovered from his illness, the old man remembered, and said, 'So you are still in Mussoorie, boy. That is good. I thought you might have gone down to Delhi to make more money.' He added that he was a little better and that he was undergoing a course of treatment at the hospital. Bisnu brought him a cup of tea and refused to take any money for it; it could be included in his own quota of free tea. When the show was over, the old man went his way and Bisnu did not see him again.

In September, the town began to get empty. The taps were running dry or giving out just a trickle of muddy water. A thick mist lay over the mountain for days on end, but there was no rain. When the mists cleared, an autumn wind came whispering through the deodars.

At the end of the month the manager of the Picture Palace gave everyone a week's notice, a week's pay, and announced that the cinema would be closing for the winter.

IV

Bali said, 'I'm going to Delhi to find work. I'll come back next summer. What about you, Bisnu, why don't you come with me? It's easier to find work in Delhi.'

'I'm staying with Chittru,' said Bisnu. 'We may work at the quarries.'

'I like the big towns,' said Bali. 'I like shops and people and lots of noise. I will never go back to my village. There is no money there, no fun.'

Bali made a bundle of his things and set out for the bus stand. Bisnu bought himself a pair of cheap shoes, for his old ones had fallen to pieces. With what was left of his money, he sent another money order home. Then he and Chittru set out for the limestone quarries, an eight-mile walk from Mussoorie.

They knew they were nearing the quarries when they saw clouds of limestone dust hanging in the air. The dust hid the next mountain from view. When they did see the mountain, they found that the top of it was missing—blasted away by dynamite to enable the quarries to get at the rich strata of limestone rock below the surface.

The skeletons of a few trees remained on the lower slopes. Almost everything else had gone—grass, flowers, shrubs, birds, butterflies, grasshoppers, ladybirds. A rock lizard popped its head out of a crevice to look at the intruders. Then, like some prehistoric survivor, it scuttled back into its underground shelter. 'I used to come here when I was small,' announced Chittru cheerfully.

'Were the quarries here then?'

'Oh, no. My friends and I—we used to come for the strawberries. They grew all over this mountain. Wild strawberries, but very tasty.'

'Where are they now?' asked Bisnu, looking around at the devastated hillside.

'All gone,' said Chittru. 'Maybe there are some on the next mountain.'

Even as they approached the quarries, a blast shook the hillside. Chittru pulled Bisnu under an overhanging rock to avoid the shower of stones that pelted down on the road. As the dust enveloped them, Bisnu had a fit of coughing. When the air cleared a little, they saw the limestone dump ahead of them.

Chittru, who was older and bigger than Bisnu, was immediately taken on as a labourer; but the quarry foreman took one look at Bisnu and said, 'You're too small. You won't be able to break stones or lift those heavy rocks and load them into the trucks. Be off, boy. Find something else to do.'

He was offered a job in the labourers' canteen, but he'd had enough of making tea and washing dishes. He was about to turn around and walk back to Mussoorie when he felt a heavy hand descend on his shoulder. He looked up to find a grey-bearded, turbanned Sikh looking down at him in some amusement.

'I need a cleaner for my truck,' he said. 'The work is easy, but the hours are long!'

Bisnu responded immediately to the man's gruff but jovial manner.

'What will you pay?' he asked.

'Fifteen rupees a day, and you'll get food and a bed at the depot.'

'As long as I don't have to cook the food,' said Bisnu.

The truck driver laughed. 'You might prefer to do so, once you've tasted the depot food. Are you coming on my truck? Make up your mind.'

'I'm your man,' said Bisnu; and waving goodbye to Chittru, he followed the Sikh to his truck.

V

A horn blared, shattering the silence of the mountains, and the truck came round a bend in the road. A herd of goats scattered left and right.

The goatherds cursed as a cloud of dust enveloped them, and then the truck had left them behind and was rattling along the bumpy, unmetalled road to the quarries.

At the wheel of the truck, stroking his grey moustache with one hand, sat Pritam Singh. It was his own truck. He had never allowed anyone else to drive it. Every day he made two trips to the quarries, carrying truckloads of limestone back to the depot at the bottom of the hill. He was paid by the trip and he was always anxious to get in two trips every day. Sitting beside him was Bisnu, his new cleaner. In less than a month, Bisnu had become an experienced hand at looking after trucks, riding in them, and even sleeping in them. He got on well with Pritam, the grizzled, fifty-year-old Sikh, who boasted two well off sons—one a farmer in Punjab, the other a wine merchant in far-off London. He could have gone to live with either of them, but his sturdy independence kept him on the road in his battered, old truck.

Pritam pressed hard on his horn. Now there was no one on the road—neither beast nor man—but Pritam was fond of the sound of his horn and liked blowing it. He boasted that it was the loudest horn in northern India. Although it struck terror into the hearts of all who heard it—for it was louder than the trumpeting of an elephant—it was music to Pritam's ears.

Pritam treated Bisnu as an equal and a friendly banter had grown between them during their many trips together.

'One more year on this bone-breaking road,' said Pritam, 'and then I'll sell my truck and retire.'

'But who will buy such a shaky old truck?' asked Bisnu. 'It will retire before you do!'

'Now don't be insulting, boy. She's only twenty years old—there are still a few years left in her!' And as though to prove it, he blew the horn again. Its strident sound echoed and re-echoed down the mountain gorge. A pair of wildfowl burst from the bushes and fled to more silent regions.

Pritam's thoughts went to his dinner. 'Haven't had a good meal for days.'

'Haven't had a good meal for weeks,' said Bisnu, although in fact he looked much healthier than when he had worked at the cinema's tea stall.

'Tonight I'll give you a dinner in a good hotel. Tandoori chicken and rice pulao.'

He sounded his horn again as though to put a seal on his promise. Then he slowed down, because the road had become narrow and precipitous, and trotting ahead of them was a train of mules.

As the horn blared, one mule ran forward, another ran backward. One went uphill, another went downhill. Soon there were mules all over the place. Pritam cursed the mules and the mule drivers cursed Pritam; but he had soon left them far behind.

Along this range, all the hills were bare and dry. Most of the forest had long since disappeared.

'Are your hills as bare as these?' asked Pritam. 'No, we still have some trees,' said Bisnu. 'Nobody has started blasting the hills as yet. In front of our house there is a walnut tree which gives us two baskets of walnuts every year. And there is an apricot tree. But it was a bad year for fruit. There was no rain. And the stream is too far away.'

'It will rain soon,' said Pritam. 'I can smell rain. It is coming from the north. The winter will be early.'

'It will settle the dust.'

Dust was everywhere. The truck was full of it. The leaves of the shrubs and the few trees were thick with it. Bisnu could feel the dust under his eyelids and in his mouth. And as they approached the quarries, the dust increased. But it was a different kind of dust now—whiter, stinging the eyes, irritating the nostrils.

They had been blasting all morning.

'Let's wait here,' said Pritam, bringing the truck to a halt. They sat in silence, staring through the windscreen at the scarred cliffs a little distance down the road. There was a sharp crack of explosives and the hillside blossomed outwards. Earth and rocks hurtled down the mountain.

Bisnu watched in awe as shrubs and small trees were flung into the air. It always frightened him—not so much the sight of the rocks bursting asunder, as the trees being flung aside and destroyed. He thought of the trees at home—the walnut, the chestnuts, the pines—and wondered if one day they would suffer the same fate, and whether the mountains would all become a desert like this particular range. No trees, no grass, no water—only the choking dust of mines and quarries.

VI

Pritam pressed hard on his horn again to let the people at the site know that he was approaching. He parked outside a small shed where the contractor and the foreman were sipping cups of tea. A short distance away, some labourers, Chittru among them, were hammering at chunks of rock, breaking them up into manageable pieces. A pile of stones stood ready for loading; while the rock that had just been blasted lay scattered about the hillside.

'Come and have a cup of tea,' called out the contractor.

'I can't hang about all day,' said Pritam. 'There's another trip to make—and the days are getting shorter. I don't want to be driving by night.'

But he sat down on a bench and ordered two cups of tea from the stall. The foreman strolled over to the group of labourers and told them to start loading. Bisnu let down the grid at the back of the truck. Then, to keep himself warm, he began helping Chittru and the men with the loading.

'Don't expect to be paid for helping,' said Sharma, the contractor, for whom every rupee spent was a rupee off his profits.

'Don't worry,' said Bisnu. 'I don't work for contractors, I work for friends.'

'That's right,' called out Pritam. 'Mind what you say to Bisnu—he's no one's servant!'

Sharma wasn't happy until there was no space left for a single stone. Then Bisnu had his cup of tea and three of the men climbed on the pile of stones in the open truck.

'All right, let's go!' said Pritam. 'I want to finish early today, Bisnu and I are having a big dinner!'

Bisnu jumped in beside Pritam, banging the door shut. It never closed properly unless it was slammed really hard. But it opened at a touch.

'This truck is held together with sticking plaster,' joked Pritam.

He was in good spirits. He started the engine, and blew his horn just as he passed the foreman and the contractor.

'They are deaf in one ear from the blasting,' said Pritam. 'I'll make them deaf in the other ear!'

The labourers were singing as the truck swung round the sharp bends of the winding road. The door beside Bisnu rattled on its hinges. He was feeling quite dizzy.

'Not too fast,' he said.

'Oh,' said Pritam. 'About my driving?'

'It's just today,' said Bisnu uneasily.

'You're getting old,' said Pritam. 'And since when did you become nervous?'

'It's a feeling, that's all.'

'That's your trouble.'

'I suppose so,' said Bisnu.

Pritam was feeling young, exhilarated. He drove faster. As they swung round a bend, Bisnu looked out of his window.

All he saw was the sky above and the valley below. They were very near the edge; but it was usually like that on this narrow mountain road.

After a few more hairpin bends, the road descended steeply to the valley. Just then a stray mule ran into the middle of the road. Pritam swung the steering wheel over to the right to avoid the mule, but here the road turned sharply to the left. The truck went over the edge.

As it tipped over, hanging for a few seconds on the edge of the cliff, the labourers leapt from the back of the truck. It pitched forward, and as it struck a rock outcrop, the loose door burst open. Bisnu was thrown out.

The truck hurtled forward, bouncing over the rocks, turning over on its side and rolling over twice before coming to rest against the trunk of a scraggly old oak tree. But for the tree, the truck would have plunged several hundred feet down to the bottom of the gorge.

Two of the labourers sat on the hillside, stunned and badly shaken. The third man had picked himself up and was running back to the quarry for help.

Bisnu had landed in a bed of nettles. He was smarting all over, but he wasn't really hurt; the nettles had broken his fall. His first impulse was to get up and run back to the road. Then he realized that Pritam was still in the truck.

Bisnu skidded down the steep slope, calling out, 'Pritam Uncle, are you all right?'

There was no answer.

VII

When Bisnu saw Pritam's arm and half his body jutting out of the open door of the truck, he feared the worst. It was a strange position, half in and half out. Bisnu was about to turn away and climb back up the hill, when he noticed that Pritam had opened a bloodied and swollen eye. It looked straight up at Bisnu.

'Are you alive?' whispered Bisnu, terrified.

'What do you think?' muttered Pritam. He closed his eye again. When the contractor and his men arrived, it took them almost an hour to get Pritam Singh out of the wreckage of the truck, and another hour to get him to the hospital in the next big town. He had broken bones, fractured ribs and a dislocated shoulder. But the doctors said he was repairable—which was more than could be said for the truck.

'So the truck's finished,' said Pritam, between groans when Bisnu came to see him after a couple of days. 'Now I'll have to go home and live with my son. And what about you, boy? I can get you a job on a friend's truck.'

'No,' said Bisnu, 'I'll be going home soon.'

'And what will you do at home?'

'I'll work on my land. It's better to grow things on the land, than to blast things out of it.'

They were silent for some time.

'There is something to be said for growing things,' said Pritam. 'But for that tree, the truck would have finished up at the foot of the mountain, and I wouldn't be here, all bandaged up and talking to you. It was the tree that saved me. Remember that, boy.'

'I'll remember, and I won't forget the dinner you promised me, either.'

It snowed during Bisnu's last night at the quarries. He slept on the floor with Chittru, in a large shed meant for the labourers. The wind blew the snowflakes in at the entrance; it whistled down the deserted mountain pass. In the morning Bisnu opened his eyes to a world of dazzling whiteness. The snow was piled high against the walls of the shed, and they had some difficulty getting out. Bisnu joined Chittru at the tea stall, drank a glass of hot, sweet tea, and ate two stale buns. He said goodbye to Chittru and set out on the long march home. The road would be closed to traffic because of the heavy snow, and he would have to walk all the way.

He trudged over the hills all day, stopping only at small villages to take refreshment. By nightfall he was still ten miles from home.

But he had fallen in with other travellers, and with them he took shelter at a small inn. They built a fire and crowded around it, and each man spoke of his home and fields and all were of the opinion that the snow and rain had come just in time to save the winter crops. Someone sang, and another told a ghost story. Feeling at home already, Bisnu fell asleep listening to their tales. In the morning, they parted and went their different ways. It was almost noon when Bisnu reached his village. The fields were covered with snow and the mountain stream was in spate. As he climbed the terraced fields to his house, he heard the sound of barking, and his mother's big black mastiff came bounding towards him over the snow. The dog jumped on him and licked his arms and then went bounding back to the house to tell the others.

Puja saw him from the courtyard and ran indoors shouting, 'Bisnu has come, my brother has come!'

His mother ran out of the house, calling, 'Bisnu, Bisnu!'

Bisnu came walking through the fields, and he did not hurry, he did not run; he wanted to savour the moment of his return, with his mother and sister smiling, waiting for him in front of the house.

There was no need to hurry now. He would be with them for a long time, and the manager of the Picture Palace would have to find someone else for the summer season... It was his home, and these were his fields! Even the snow was his. When the snow melted, he would clear the fields, and nourish them, and make them rich.

He felt very big and very strong as he came striding over the land he loved.

WILD FLOWERS NEAR A MOUNTAIN STREAM

Below my house is a forest of oak and maple and Himalayan rhododendron. A path twists its way down through the trees, over an open ridge where red sorrel grows wild, and then steeply down through a tangle of thorn bushes, vines and rangal bamboo. At the bottom of the hill the path leads on to a grassy verge, surrounded by wild rose. A stream runs close by the verge, tumbling over smooth pebbles, over rocks worn yellow with age, on its way to the plains and the little Song River and finally to the sacred Ganges.

When I first discovered the stream, it was April and the wild roses were flowering, small white blossoms lying in clusters. There were primroses on the hill slopes, and an occasional late-flowering rhododendron provided a splash of red against the dark green of the hill.

The St John's Wort was flowering profusely on small shrubs.

Many legends have grown around this flower of pure dazzling sunshine which takes its family name—Hypericaceae—from the great Titan god Hyperion, who was the father of the Greek God of the sun, Apollo.

Is a friend of yours insane? Then get him to drink the sap from the leaves and stalks of the St John's Wort. He will be well again.

Are you hurt? If your wounds do not heal, take the juice and put it on the wound; and if the bleeding will not stop, take more juice.

Is your father bald? Then he must rise early one morning and bathe his head with the dew from St John's Wort, and his hair will grow again.

Do you live on the Isle of Man? Then beware! Tread not on the St John's Wort after sunset, lest a fairy horseman arise and carry you off. He will land you anywhere.

These are all English or Irish superstitions, but the St John's Wort is as profuse in the lower ranges of the Himalayas as it is anywhere in Europe.

A spotted forktail, a bird of the Himalayan streams, was much in evidence during those early visits. It moved nimbly over the boulders with a fairy tread, and continually wagged its tail.

In May and June, when the hills are always brown and dry, it remained cool and green near the stream, where ferns and maidenhair and long grasses continued to thrive. Downstream I found a cave with water dripping from the roof, the water spangled gold and silver in the shafts of sunlight that pushed through the slits in the cave roof. Few people came there. Sometimes a milkman or a coal-burner would cross the stream on his way to a village; but the nearby hill station's summer visitors had not discovered this haven of wild and green things.

The monkeys—langurs, with white and silver-grey fur, black faces and long swishing tails—had discovered the place, but they kept to the trees and sunlit slopes. They grew quite accustomed to my presence, and carried on with their work and play as though I did not exist. The young ones scuffled and wrestled like boys, while their parents attended to each other's toilets, stretching themselves out on the grass, beautiful animals with slim waists and long sinewy legs, and tails full of character. They were clean and polite, much nicer than the red monkeys of the plains.

During the rains, the stream became a rushing torrent, bushes and small trees were swept away, and the friendly murmur of the water became a threatening boom. I did not visit the spot very often. There were leeches in the long grass, and they would fasten themselves on to my legs and feast on my blood. But it was always worthwhile tramping through the forest to feast my eyes on the foliage that sprang up in tropical profusion—soft, spongy moss; great stag ferns on the trunks of trees; mysterious and sometimes evil-looking orchids; the climbing convolvulus opening its purple secrets to the morning sun; and the wood sorrel, or oxalis—so named because of the oxalic acid derived from its roots—with its clover-like leaflets, which fold down like umbrellas at the first sign of rain.

And then, after a November hailstorm, it was winter, and one could not lie on the frostbitten grass. The sound of the stream was the same, but I missed the birds.

It snowed—the snow lay heavy on the branches of the oak trees and piled up in the culverts—and the grass and the ferns and wild flowers were pressed to sleep beneath a cold white blanket; but the stream flowed on, pushing its way through and under the whiteness, towards another river, towards another spring.

BIRDSONG IN THE HILLS

Birdwatching is more difficult in the hills than on the plains. Many birds are difficult to spot against the dark green of the trees or the varying shades of the hillsides. Large gardens and open fields make birdwatching much easier on the plains; but up here in the mountains one has to be quick of eye to spot a flycatcher flitting from tree to tree, or a mottled brown tree creeper ascending the trunk of oak or spruce. But few birds remain silent, and one learns of their presence from their calls or songs. Birdsong is with you wherever you go in the hills, from the foothills to the tree line; and it is often easier to recognize a bird from its voice than from its colourful but brief appearance.

The barbet is one of those birds which are heard more than they are seen. Summer visitors to our hill stations must have heard their monotonous, far-reaching call, *pee-oh*, *pee-oh*, or *un-neeow*, *un-neeow*. They would probably not have seen the birds, as they keep to the tops of high trees where they are not easily distinguished from the foliage. Apart from that, the sound carries for about half a mile, and as the bird has the habit of turning its head from side to side while calling, it is very difficult to know in which direction to look for it.

Barbets love listening to their own voices and often two or three birds answer each other from different trees, each trying to outdo the other in a shrill shouting match. Most birds are noisy during the mating season. Barbets are noisy all the year round!

Some people like the barbet's call and consider it both striking and pleasant. Some don't like it and simply consider it striking!

In parts of the Garhwal Himalayas, there is a legend that the bird is the reincarnation of a moneylender who died of grief at the unjust termination of a lawsuit. Eternally his plaint rises to heaven, *un-neeow, un-neeow* which means, 'injustice, injustice'.

Barbets are found throughout the tropical world, but probably the finest of these birds is the great Himalayan barbet. Just over a foot in length, it has a massive yellow bill, almost as large as that of a toucan. The head and neck are a rich violet; the upper back is olive brown with pale green streaks. The wings are green, washed with blue, brown and yellow. In spite of all these brilliant colours, the barbet is not easily distinguished from its leafy surroundings. It goes for the highest treetops and seldom comes down to earth.

Hodgson's grey-headed flycatcher-warbler is the long name that ornithologists, in their infinite wisdom, have given to a very small bird. This tiny bird is heard, if not seen, more often than any other bird throughout the Western Himalayas. It is almost impossible to visit any hill station between Naini Tal and Dalhousie without noticing this warbler; its voice is heard in every second tree; and yet there are few who can say what it looks like.

Its song (if you can call it that) is not very musical, and Douglas Dewar in writing about it was reminded of a notice that once appeared in a third-rate music hall: The audience is respectfully requested not to throw things at the pianist. He is doing his best.

Our little warbler does his best, incessantly emitting four or five unmusical but joyful and penetrating notes.

He is much smaller than a sparrow, being only some four inches in length, of which one-third consists of tail. His lower plumage is bright yellow, his upper parts olive green; the head and neck are grey, the head being set off by cream-coloured eyebrows. He is an active little bird always on the move, and both he and his mate, and sometimes a few friends, hop about from leaf to leaf, looking for insects both large and small. And the way he puts away an inch-long caterpillar would please the most accomplished spaghetti eater!

Another tiny bird heard more often than it is seen is the green-backed tit, a smart little bird about the size of a sparrow. It constantly utters a sharp, rather metallic but not unpleasant, call which sounds like 'kiss me, kiss me, kiss me…'

Another fine singer is the sunbird, which is found in Kumaon and Garhwal. But perhaps the finest songster is the grey-winged ouzel. Throughout the early summer he makes the wooded hillsides ring with his blackbird-like melody. The hill people call this bird the kastura or kasturi, a name also applied to the Himalayan whistling thrush. But the whistling thrush has a yellow bill, whereas the ouzel is redbilled and is much the sweeter singer.

Nightjars (or goatsuckers, to give them their ancient name) are birds that lie concealed during the day in shady woods, coming out at dusk on silent wings to hunt for insects. The nightjar has a huge frog-like mouth, but is best recognized by its long tail and wings and its curiously silent flight. After dusk and just before dawn, you can hear its curious call, *tonk-tonk, tonk-tonk*—a note like that produced by striking a plank with a hammer.

As we pass from the plains to the hills, the traveller is transported from one bird realm to another.

Rajpur is separated from Mussoorie by a five-mile footpath, and within that brief distance we find the caw of the house crow replaced by the deeper note of the corby. Instead of the crescendo shriek of the koel, the double note of the cuckoo meets the ear. For the eternal cooing of the little brown dove, the melodious kokla green pigeon is substituted. The harsh cries of the rose-ringed parakeets give place to the softer call of the slate-headed species. The dissonant voices of the seven-sisters no longer issue from the bushes; their place is taken by the weird but more pleasing calls of the Himalayan streaked laughing thrushes.

When I first came to live in the hills, it was the song of the Himalayan whistling thrush that caught my attention. I did not see the bird that day. It kept to the deep shadows of the ravine below the old stone cottage.

The following day I was sitting at my window, gazing out at the new leaves on the walnut and wild pear trees. All was still, the wind was at peace with itself, the mountains brooded massively under the darkening sky. And then, emerging from the depths of that sunless chasm like a dark sweet secret, came the indescribably beautiful call of the whistling thrush.

It is a song that never fails to thrill and enchant me. The bird starts with a hesitant schoolboy whistle, as though trying out the tune; then, confident of the melody, it bursts into full song, a crescendo of sweet notes and variations that ring clearly across the hillside. Suddenly the song breaks off right in the middle of a cadenza, and I am left wondering what happened to make the bird stop so suddenly.

At first the bird was heard but never seen. Then one day I found the whistling thrush perched on the broken garden fence. He was deep glistening purple, his shoulders flecked with white; he had sturdy black legs and a strong yellow beak. A dapper fellow who would have looked just right in a tophat! When he saw me coming down the path, he uttered a sharp *kree-ee*—unexpectedly harsh when compared to his singing—and flew off into the shadowed ravine.

As the months passed, he grew used to my presence and became less shy. Once the rainwater pipes were blocked, and this resulted in an overflow of water and a small permanent puddle under the steps. This became the whistling thrush's favourite bathing place. On sultry summer afternoons, while I was taking a siesta upstairs, I would hear the bird flapping about in the rainwater pool. A little later, refreshed and sunning himself on the roof, he would treat me to a little concert—performed, I could not help feeling, especially for my benefit.

It was Govind, the milkman, who told me the legend of the whistling thrush, locally called kastura by the hill people, but also going by the name of Krishan-patti.

According to the story, Lord Krishna fell asleep near a mountain stream and while he slept, a small boy made off with the god's famous flute. Upon waking and finding his flute gone, Krishna was so angry that he changed the culprit into a bird. But having once played on the flute, the bird had learnt bits and pieces of Krishna's wonderful music. And so he continued, in his disrespectful way, to play the music of the gods, only stopping now and then (as the whistling thrush does) when he couldn't remember the tune.

It wasn't long before my whistling thrush was joined by a female, who looked exactly like him. (I am sure there are subtle points of difference, but not to my myopic eyes!) Sometimes they gave solo performances, sometimes they sang duets; and these, no doubt, were love calls, because it wasn't long before the pair were making forays into the rocky ledges of the ravine, looking for a suitable maternity home. But a few breeding seasons were to pass before I saw any of their young.

After almost three years in the hills, I came to the conclusion that these were 'birds for all seasons'. They were liveliest in midsummer; but even in the depths of winter, with snow lying on the ground, they would suddenly start singing as they flitted from pine to oak to naked chestnut.

As I write, there is a strong wind rushing through the trees and bustling about in the chimney, while distant thunder threatens a storm. Undismayed, the whistling thrushes are calling to each other as they roam the wind-threshed forest.

Whistling thrushes usually nest on rocky ledges near water; but my overtures of friendship may give my visitors other ideas. Recently I was away from Mussoorie for about a fortnight. When I returned, I was about to open the window when I noticed a large bundle of ferns, lichen, grass, mud and moss balanced outside on the window ledge. Peering through the glass, I was able to recognize this untidy bundle as a nest.

It meant, of course, that I couldn't open the window, as this would have resulted in the nest toppling over the edge. Fortunately the room had another window and I kept this one open to let in sunshine, fresh air, the music of birds, and, always welcome, the call of the postman! The postman's call may not be as musical as birdsong, but this writer never tires of it, for it heralds the arrival of the occasional cheque that makes it possible for him to live close to nature.

And now, this very day, three pink freckled eggs lie in the cup of moss that forms the nursery in this jumble of a nest. The parent birds, both male and female, come and go, bustling about very efficiently, fully prepared for a great day that's coming soon.

The wild cherry tree, which I grew especially for birds, attract a great many small birds, both when it is in flower and when it is in fruit.

When it is covered with pale pink blossoms, the most common visitor is a little yellow-backed sunbird, who emits a squeaky little song as he flits from branch to branch. He extracts the nectar from the blossoms with his tubular tongue, sometimes while hovering on the wing but usually while clinging to the slender twigs.

Just as some vegetarians will occasionally condescend to eat meat, the sunbird (like the barbet) will vary his diet with insects. Small spiders, caterpillars, beetles, bugs and flies (probably in most cases themselves visitors to these flowers) fall prey to these birds. I have also seen a sunbird flying up and catching insects on the wing.

The flycatchers are gorgeous birds, especially the paradise flycatcher with its long white tail and ghostlike flight; and although they are largely insectivorous, like some meat-eaters they will also take a little fruit! And so they will occasionally visit the cherry tree when its sour little cherries are ripening. While travelling over the boughs, they utter twittering notes with occasional louder calls, and now and then the male bird breaks out into a sweet little song, thus justifying the name of shah bulbul by which he is known in northern India.

BREAKFAST AT BAROG

It's well over seventy years that I actually breakfasted at Barog, that little railway station on the Kalka–Simla line, but last night I dreamt of it—dreamt of the station, the dining room, the hillside and the long dark Barog tunnel—which meant that it had been present in my subconscious all these years and was now striving to come to the fore and revive a few poignant memories.

Should I go there again? The station is still there, and so is the tunnel. I'm told that the area has been built up over the years, so that it is now almost a mini hill station. That wouldn't surprise me. Our villages have become towns, our towns have become cities and in a few years' time our country will be one vast megacity with a few parks here and there to remind us that this was once a green planet.

I don't remember any dwellings around Barog, just that one little station and its one little restaurant with a cook and a waiter and its one little stationmaster. No, such a small station couldn't have had someone as important as a stationmaster. Someone quite junior must have been in charge.

Never mind. It was the breakfast that was important. And that I was with my father and on my way to Simla and a boarding school. The boarding school was the least desirable part of the journey. It was almost two years since I had been in a school and I was perfectly happy to continue living in an ideal world where schools need not exist. The breakup of my parents' marriage had resulted in my being withdrawn from a convent school in Mussoorie and taken over by my father who was on active service with the RAF. It was 1942 and World War II was at its peak. Against all regulations he kept me with him, but to do this he had to rent a flat in New Delhi. Most of the day he was at work and I would have the flat to myself, surrounded by books, gramophone records and stamp albums. Evenings I would help him with his stamp collection, for he was an avid collector. On weekends he would take me to see Delhi's historic monuments; there was no dearth of them. From the stamps I learnt geography, from the monuments history, from the books literature. I learnt more in two years at home than I did in a year at school.

But finally he was transferred—first Colombo, then Karachi, then Calcutta—and it was no longer possible for me to share his quarters. I was admitted to Bishop Cotton's in Simla.

We took the railcar from Kalka. It glided over the rails without any of the huffing and puffing of the steam engine that dragged the little narrow gauge train up the steep mountain. I would be travelling in that train in the years to come, but on this, my first to Simla, I was given the luxury of the railcar.

It glided into the Barog station punctually at 10 a.m., in time for breakfast.

The Barog breakfast was already well known and I did full justice to it. I skipped the cornflakes and concentrated on the scrambled eggs and buttered toasts. There was bacon too, and honey and marmalade.

'Tuck in, Ruskin,' said my father, 'School breakfasts won't be half as good.'

He didn't eat much himself. There was a lot on his mind in those days, apart from his work. There was his estranged wife, my mother; my invalid sister, now with his mother in Calcutta; his frequent transfers; his own frequent attacks of malaria; and our future in India, once the War was over—for India's Independence was just around the corner.

'When do we get to Simla?' I asked, quite happy to remain in Barog forever.

'In a little over an hour. But first we go through the longest of all the tunnels on this line. It will take about five minutes. Time for you to make a wish.'

The railcar plunged into the tunnel and we were enveloped in the darkness of the mountain. I held my father's hand. A couple of soldiers sitting behind us broke into a song from an earlier war.

'Pack up your troubles in your old kitbag,
And smile, smile, smile!'

A glimmer of daylight appeared at the end of the tunnel and then we were out in the sunshine and the pine-scented air.

'Did you make your wish?' asked my father.

I nodded, 'I wished that my mother would come back.'

He was silent for a few moments. 'Do you miss her a lot?'

'I don't miss her,' I said firmly. 'I'm always happy with you. But you miss her all the time. I don't like to see you so sad.'

'I've often asked her to come back,' he said. 'But it's up to her. She wants a different kind of life.'

And that was true. She was still very young—in her late twenties—and she enjoyed parties and dances and a busy social life. My father was in his forties. He liked staying at home, listening to classical music. When he took a holiday, he went in search of rare butterflies. My mother was a butterfly too—pretty, merry, fluttering here and there—but most unwilling to be displayed in a butterfly museum.

I suppose, for most of us, big or small, life is just a succession of making mistakes and we spend most of our time trying to rectify them. Marriage was a mistake for both my parents. And I was a product of that mistake!

In the time he had, my father did his best for me. And how proud I was of him when he accompanied me down to my new school! He was wearing his dark blue RAF uniform with its flying officer's stripes, and uniforms, especially officers' uniforms, made a great impression amongst schoolboys in those wartime days. I was received with respect and curiosity. Word went around that my father was a fighter pilot and that he'd shot down dozens of Japanese planes! He was another Biggles, that fictional aviator. Nothing could have been further from reality. My father did not fly at all. He worked for a unit called Codes and Cyphers, helping to create new codes or breaking down enemy codes. It was important work and secret work but there was no glamour about it.

Not that I was averse to the glamour of being Biggles Junior. In my previous school, I'd been something of an outsider and the Irish nuns hadn't cared much for a quiet, sensitive boy. Here I was made to feel I belonged and in no time at all I made a number of friends. It was already halfway through the school year but I had no difficulty in catching up with my classmates.

This was 'prep' school—junior school—and certainly more fun than senior school, still a couple of years away, would ever be... Still, I was always looking forward to the winter break, when I would be with my father again, for at least three months. And there he was, waiting at the Old Delhi railway station, as my train drew alongside the platform. He was still in Delhi, at Air Headquarters, and I made the most of my time with him. Connaught Place was close by, and two or three evenings every week, we would go to the cinema. There were four to choose from—the Regal, the Rivoli, the Odeon and the Plaza—all very new and smart and showing the latest films from Hollywood. I became a regular film buff. The bookshops were there too, and the record shops and Wenger's with its confectionery and the Milk Bar with its milkshakes and Kwality with its ice creams. It was hard to believe that there was a world war going on in Europe and Asia and North Africa and the Pacific; or that the Quit India movement was at its height and that my father and I might have to leave the country in the near future. He spoke about it sometimes and of the possibility of my going to a school in England. We did not talk about my mother, but I noticed that he still kept a photograph of her in his desk drawer.

It was back to school in March, when the rhododendrons were in bloom. This time I went up with the school party, in the small train with its steam engine chugging slowly up the steep inclines. The journey took all day. We did stop briefly at Barog, but we were not allowed to get down from the train; one or two boys were certain to be left behind. I looked longingly at the little restaurant on the far side of the platform; but it was already teatime. Breakfast was for the railcar!

The school year rolled on. My father was transferred to Karachi and then to Calcutta. He had grown up in Calcutta and knew the city well. He wrote to me every week and in his last letter he told me what I could look forward to during the winter holidays—the New Market with its bookshops, the botanical gardens with its ancient banyan tree, the zoo, the riverfront, the great maidan where hundreds of people would be taking in the evening air... I was hoping he would come up to see me during the autumn break, but instead I had news of another kind.

It must be difficult for a young schoolmaster, as yet untouched by tragedy, to tell a ten-year-old that he has just lost his father. Mr Murtough was given this onerous duty. And he did his best, mumbling something ridiculous about God needing my father more than I did and so on and so on...

My friends were more natural in expressing this sympathy—giving me their sweets or chocolates, offering to play games with me, talking to me in the middle of the night when they discovered I wasn't asleep... For the future did look bleak. I wasn't sure where I would be going next—my Calcutta granny or my Dehra granny, or my mother and stepfather... I did receive a letter from my mother, telling me that my father had died of the malaria that had plagued him for years; but it was an unemotional letter and it did little to bring me comfort.

But I did go to her when school closed for the winter and I was to spend the next few years in my stepfather's home. But that's another story.

I continued my school in Simla, and every year in March, the small train would take me and my schoolmates up the mountain, through numerous tunnels and winding gradients, forests of pine and deodar, and we always stopped at Barog, before the biggest tunnel of all. But I never made another wish when passing through that tunnel.

That was over seventy years ago.

Is the railcar still running on that line? And do they still serve breakfast at Barog?

They say you should see Venice before you die. Or better

still, Varanasi. But I'll settle for that little station among the pines. And if my father is standing on the platform, waiting for me, ready to take me by the hand, I'll be a small boy again and that railcar will take us to a different destination altogether.

COLD BEER AT CHHUTMALPUR

Just outside the small market town of Chhutmalpur (on the way back from Delhi) one is greeted by a large signboard with just two words on it: Cold Beer. The signboard is almost as large as the shop from which the cold beer is dispensed; but after a gruelling five-hour drive from Delhi, in the heat and dust of May, a glass of chilled beer is welcome—except, of course, to teetotallers who will find other fizzy ways to satiate their thirst.

Chhutmalpur is not the sort of place you'd choose to retire in. But it has its charms, not the least of which is its Sunday Market, when the varied produce of the rural interior finds its way on to the dusty pavements, and the air vibrates with noise, colour and odours. Carpets of red chillies, seasonal fruits, stacks of grain and vegetables, cheap toys for the children, bangles of lac, wooden artifacts, colourful underwear, sweets of every description, *churan* to go with them...

'*Lakar hajam, gather hajam!*' cries the churan-seller. Translated: Digest wood, digest stones! That is, if you partake of this particular digestive pill which, when I tried it, appeared to be one part *hing* (asafoetida) and one part gunpowder. Things are seldom what they seem to be. Passing through the small town of Purkazi, I noticed a sign-board which announced the availability of 'Books'—just that. Intrigued, I stopped to find out more about this bookshop in the wilderness. Perhaps I'd find a rare tome to add to my library. Peeping in, I discovered that the dark interior was stacked from floor to ceiling with exercise books! Apparently the shop-owner was the supplier for the district.

Rare books can be seen in Roorkee, in the University's old library. Here, not many years ago, a First Folio Shakespeare turned up and was celebrated in the Indian Press as a priceless discovery. Perhaps it's still there.

Also in the library is a bust of Sir Proby Cautley, who conceived and built the Ganga Canal, which starts at Haridwar and passes through Roorkee on its way across the Doab. Hardly anyone today has heard of Cautley, and yet surely his achievement outstrips that of many Englishmen in India—soldiers and statesmen who became famous for doing all the wrong things.

Cautley's Canal

Cautley came to India at the age of seventeen and joined the Bengal Artillery. In 1825, he assisted Captain Robert Smith, the engineer in charge of constructing the Eastern Yamuna Canal. By 1836 he was Superintendent-General of Canals. From the start, he worked towards his dream of building a Ganga Canal, and spent six months walking and riding through the jungles and countryside, taking each level and measurement himself, sitting up all night to transfer them to his maps. He was confident that a 500-kilometre canal was feasible. There were many objections and obstacles to his project, most of them financial, but Cautley persevered and eventually persuaded the East India Company to back him.

Digging of the canal began in 1839. Cautley had to make his own bricks—millions of them—his own brick kiln, and his own mortar. A hundred thousand tonnes of lime went into the mortar, the other main ingredient of which was *surkhi*, made by grinding over-burnt bricks to a powder. To reinforce the mortar, *ghur*, ground lentils and jute fibres were added to it.

Initially, opposition came from the priests in Haridwar, who felt that the waters of the holy Ganga would be imprisoned. Cautley pacified them by agreeing to leave a narrow gap in the dam through which the river water could flow unchecked. He won over the priests when he inaugurated his project with aarti, and the worship of Ganesh, god of good beginnings. He also undertook the repair of the sacred bathing ghats along the river. The canal banks were also to have their own ghats with steps leading down to the water.

The headworks of the canal are at Haridwar, where the Ganga enters the plains after completing its majestic journey through the Himalayas. Below Haridwar, Cautley had to dig new courses for some of the mountain torrents that threatened the canal. He collected them into four steams and took them over the canal by means of four passages. Near Roorkee, the land fell away sharply and here Cautley had to build an aqueduct, a masonry bridge that carries the canal for half a kilometre across the Solani torrent—a unique engineering feat. At Roorkee, the canal is twenty-five metres higher than the parent river which flows almost parallel to it.

Most of the excavation work on the canal was done mainly by the Oads, a gypsy tribe who were professional diggers for most of northwest India. They took great pride in their work. Though extremely poor, Cautley found them a happy and carefree lot who worked in a very organized manner.

When the canal was formally opened on 8 April 1854, its main channel was 348 miles long, its branches 306 and the distributaries over 3,000. Over 767,000 acres in 5,000 villages were irrigated. One of its main branches re-entered the Ganga at Kanpur; it also had branches to Fatehgarh, Bulandshahr and Aligarh.

Cautley's achievements did not end there. He was also actively involved in Dr Falconer's fossil expedition in the Siwaliks. He presented to the British Museum an extensive collection of fossil mammalia—including hippopotamus and crocodile fossils, evidence that the region was once swampland or an inland sea. Other animal remains found here included the sabre-toothed tiger; Elephis ganesa, an elephant with a trunk ten-and-a-half feet long; a three-toed ancestor of the horse; the bones of a fossil ostrich; and the remains of giant cranes and tortoises. Exciting times, exciting finds.

Nor did Cautley's interests and activities end in fossil excavation. My copy of Surgeon General Balfour's Cyclopedia of India (1873) lists a number of fascinating reports and papers by Cautley. He wrote on a submerged city, twenty feet underground, near Behut in the Doab; on the coal and lignite in the Himalayas; on gold washings in the Siwalik Hills, between the Jamuna and Sutlej rivers; on a new species of snake; on the mastodons of the Siwaliks; on the manufacture of tar; and on Panchukkis or corn mills.

How did he find time for all this, I wonder. Most of his life was spent in tents, overseeing the canal work or digging up fossils. He had a house in Mussoorie (one of the first), but he could not have spent much time in it. It is today part of the Manav Bharti School, and there is still a plaque in the office stating that Cautley lived there. Perhaps he wrote some of his reports and expositions during brief sojourns in the hills. It is said that his wife left him, unable to compete against the rival attractions of canals and fossils remains.

I wonder, too, if there was any follow up on his reports of the submerged city—is it still there, waiting to be re-discovered—or his findings on gold washings in the Siwaliks. Should my royalties ever dry up, I might just wonder off into the Siwaliks, looking for 'gold in them that hills'. Meanwhile, whenever I travel by road from Delhi to Haridwar, and pass over that placid canal at various places en-route, I think of the man who spent more than twenty years of his life in executing this magnificent project, and others equally demanding. And then, his work done, walking away from it all without thought of fame or fortune.

A Jungle Princess

From Roorkee separate roads lead to Haridwar, Saharanpur, Dehradun. And from the Saharanpur road, you can branch off to Paonta Sahib, with its famous gurdwara glistening above the blue waters of the Yamuna. Still blue up here, but not so blue by the time it enters Delhi. Industrial affluents and human waste soon muddy the purest of rivers.

From Paonta you can turn right to Herbertpur, a small township originally settled by an Anglo-Indian family early in the nineteenth century. As may be inferred by its name, Herbert was the scion of the family, but I have been unable to discover much about him. When I was a boy, the Carberry family owned much of the land around here, but by the time Independence came, only one of the family remained—Doreen, a sultry, dusky beauty who become known in Dehra as the 'Jungle Princess'. Her husband had deserted her, but she had a small daughter who grew up on the land. Doreen's income came from her mango and guava orchards, and she seemed quite happy living in this isolated rural area near the river. Occasionally she came into Dehradun, a bus ride of a couple of hours, and she would visit my mother, a childhood friend, and occasionally stay overnight.

On one occasion, we went to Doreen's jungle home for a couple of days. I was just seven or eight years old. I remember Doreen's daughter (about my age) teaching me to climb trees. I managed the guava tree quite well, but some of the others were too difficult for me.

How did this jungle queen manage to live by herself in this remote area, where her house, orchard and fields were bordered by forest on one side and the river on the other?

Well, she had her servants of course, and they were loyal to her. And she also possessed several guns, and could handle them very well. I saw her bring down a couple of pheasants with her twelve-bore spread shot. She had also killed a cattle-lifting tiger which had been troubling a nearby village, and a marauding leopard that had taken one of her dogs. So she was quite capable of taking care of herself. When I last saw her, some twenty-five years ago, she was in her seventies. I believe she sold her land and went to live elsewhere with her daughter, who by then had a family of her own.

SOUNDS I LIKE TO HEAR

All night the rain has been drumming on the corrugated tin roof. There has been no storm, no thunder, just the steady swish of a tropical downpour. It helps one to lie awake; at the same time, it doesn't keep one from sleeping.

It is a good sound to read by—the rain outside, the quiet within—and, although tin roofs are given to springing unaccountable leaks, there is in general a feeling of being untouched by, and yet in touch with, the rain.

Gentle rain on a tin roof is one of my favourite sounds. And early in the morning, when the rain has stopped, there are other sounds I like to hear—a crow shaking the raindrops from his feathers and cawing rather disconsolately; babblers and bulbuls bustling in and out of bushes and long grass in search of worms and insects; the sweet, ascending trill of the Himalayan whistling thrush; dogs rushing through damp undergrowth.

A cherry tree, bowed down by the heavy rain, suddenly rights itself, flinging pellets of water in my face.

Some of the best sounds are made by water. The water of a mountain stream, always in a hurry, bubbling over rocks and chattering, 'I'm late, I'm late!' like the White Rabbit, tumbling over itself in its anxiety to reach the bottom of the hill, the sound of the sea, especially when it is far away—or when you hear it by putting a seashell to your ear. The sound made by dry and thirsty earth, as it sucks at a sprinkling of water. Or the sound of a child drinking thirstily, the water running down his chin and throat.

Water gushing out of the pans of an old well outside a village while a camel moves silently round the well. Bullock-cart wheels creaking over rough country roads. The clip-clop of a pony carriage, and the tinkle of its bell, and the singsong call of its driver...

Bells in the hills. A school bell ringing, and children's voices drifting through an open window. A temple bell, heard faintly from across the valley. Heavy silver ankle bells on the feet of sturdy hill women. Sheep bells heard high up on the mountainside.

Do falling petals make a sound? Just the tiniest and softest of sounds, like the drift of falling snow. Of course big flowers, like dahlias, drop their petals with a very definite flop. These are show-offs, like the hawk moth who comes flapping into the rooms at night instead of emulating the butterfly dipping lazily on the afternoon breeze.

One must return to the birds for favourite sounds, and the birds of the plains differ from the birds of the hills. On a cold winter morning in the plains of northern India, if you walk some way into the jungle you will hear the familiar call of the black partridge: *'Bhagwan teri qudrat'* it seems to cry, which means: 'Oh God! Great is thy might.'

The cry rises from the bushes in all directions; but an hour later not a bird is to be seen or heard and the jungle is so very still that the silence seems to shout at you.

There are sounds that come from a distance, beautiful

because they are far away, voices on the wind—they 'walketh upon the wings of the wind'. The cries of fishermen out on the river. Drums beating rhythmically in a distant village. The croaking of frogs from the rainwater pond behind the house. I mean frogs at a distance. A frog croaking beneath one's window is as welcome as a motor horn.

But some people like motor horns. I know a taxi driver who never misses an opportunity to use his horn. It was made to his own specifications, and it gives out a resonant bugle call. He never tires of using it. Cyclists and pedestrians always scatter at his approach. Other cars veer off the road. He is proud of his horn. He loves its strident sound—which only goes to show that some men's sounds are other men's noises!

Homely sounds, though we don't often think about them, are the ones we miss most when they are gone. A kettle on the boil. A door that creaks on its hinges. Old sofa springs. Familiar voices lighting up the dark. Ducks quacking in the rain.

And so we return to the rain, with which my favourite sounds began.

I have sat out in the open at night, after a shower of rain when the whole air is murmuring and tinkling with the voices of crickets and grasshoppers and little frogs. There is one melodious sound, a sweet repeated trill, which I have never been able to trace to its source. Perhaps it is a little tree frog. Or it may be a small green cricket. I shall never know.

I am not sure that I really want to know. In an age when a scientific and rational explanation has been given for almost everything we see and touch and hear, it is good to be left with one small mystery, a mystery sweet and satisfying and entirely my own.

Listen!

Listen to the night wind in the trees,
Listen to the summer grass singing;
Listen to the time that's tripping by,
And the dawn dew falling.
Listen to the moon as it climbs the sky,
Listen to the pebbles humming;
Listen to the mist in the trembling leaves,
And the silence calling.

LANDOUR BAZAAR

In most North Indian bazaars, there is a clock tower. And like most clocks in clock towers, this one works in fits and starts: listless in summer, sluggish during the monsoon, stopping altogether when it snows in January. Almost every year the tall brick structure gets a coat of paint. It was pink last year. Now it's a livid purple.

From the clock tower at one end to the mule sheds at the other, this old Mussoorie bazaar is a mile long. The tall, shaky three-storey buildings cling to the mountainside, shutting out the sunlight. They are even shakier now that heavy trucks have started rumbling down the narrow street, originally made for nothing heavier than a rickshaw. The street is narrow and damp, retaining all the bazaar smells—sweetmeats frying, smoke from wood or charcoal fires, the sweat and urine of mules, petrol fumes, all these mingle with the smell of mist and old buildings and distant pines.

The bazaar sprang up about 150 years ago to serve the needs of British soldiers who were sent to the Landour convalescent depot to recover from sickness or wounds. The old military hospital, built in 1827, now houses the Defence Institute of

Work Study.* One old resident of the bazaar, a ninety-year-old tailor, can remember the time, in the early years of the century, when the Redcoats marched through the small bazaar on their way to the cantonment church. And they always carried their rifles into church, remembering how many had been surprised in churches during the 1857 uprising.

Today, the Landour bazaar serves the local population, Mussoorie itself being more geared to the needs and interest of tourists. There are a number of silversmiths in Landour. They fashion silver nose-rings, earrings, bracelets and anklets, which are bought by the women from the surrounding Jaunpuri villages. One silversmith had a chest full of old silver rupees. These rupees are sometimes hung on thin silver chains and worn as pendants. I have often seen women in Garhwal wearing pendants or necklaces of rupees embossed with the profiles of Queen Victoria or King Edward VII.

At the other extreme, there are the kabari shops, where you can pick up almost everything—a tape recorder discarded by a Woodstock student, or a piece of furniture from Grandmother's time in the hill station. Old clothes, Victorian bric-a-brac, and bits of modern gadgetry vie for your attention.

The old clothes are often more reliable than the new. Last winter I bought a new pullover marked 'Made in Nepal' from a Tibetan pavement vendor. I was wearing it on the way home when it began to rain. By the time I reached my cottage, the pullover had shrunk inches and I had some difficulty getting out of it! It was now just the right size for Bijju, the milkman's twelve-year-old son, and I gave it to the boy. But it continued

---

*The Defence Institute of Work Study has been renamed the Institute of Technology Management.

to shrink at every wash, and it is now being worn by Teju, Bijju's younger brother, who is eight.

At the dark windy corner in the bazaar, one always found an old man hunched up over his charcoal fire, roasting peanuts. He'd been there for as long as I could remember, and he could be seen at almost any hour of the day or night, in all weathers.

He was probably quite tall, but I never saw him standing up. One judged his height from his long, loose limbs. He was very thin, probably tubercular, and the high cheekbones added to the tautness of his tightly stretched skin.

His peanuts were always fresh, crisp and hot. They were popular with small boys, who had a few coins to spend on their way to and from school. On cold winter evenings, there was always a demand for peanuts from people of all ages.

No one seemed to know the old man's name. No one had ever thought of asking. One just took his presence for granted. He was as fixed a landmark as the clock tower or the old cherry tree that grew crookedly from the hillside. He seemed less perishable than the tree, more dependable than the clock. He had no family, but in a way all the world was his family because he was in continuous contact with people. And yet he was a remote sort of being; always polite, even to children, but never familiar. He was seldom alone, but he must have been lonely.

Summer nights he rolled himself up in a thin blanket and slept on the ground beside the dying embers of his fire. During winter he waited until the last cinema show was over, before retiring to the rickshaw-coolies' shelter where there was protection from the freezing wind.

Did he enjoy being alive? I often wondered. He was not a joyful person; but then neither was he miserable. Perhaps he was one of those who do not attach much importance to themselves, who are emotionally uninvolved in the life around them, content with their limitations, their dark corners; people on whom cares rest lightly, simply because they do not care at all.

I wanted to get to know the old man better, to sound him out on the immense questions involved in roasting peanuts all one's life; but it's too late now. He died last summer.

That corner remained very empty, very dark, and every time I passed it, I was haunted by visions of the old peanut vendor, troubled by the questions I did not ask; and I wondered if he was really as indifferent to life as he appeared to be.

Then, a few weeks ago, there was a new occupant of the corner, a new seller of peanuts. No relative of the old man, but a boy of thirteen or fourteen. The human personality can impose its own nature on its surroundings. In the old man's time it seemed a dark, gloomy corner. Now it's lit up by sunshine—a sunny personality, smiling, chattering. Old age gives way to youth; and I'm glad I won't be alive when the new peanut vendor grows old. One shouldn't see too many people grow old.

Leaving the main bazaar behind, I walk some way down the Mussoorie–Tehri road, a fine road to walk on, in spite of the dust from an occasional bus or jeep. From Mussoorie to Chamba, a distance of some thirty-five miles, the road seldom descends below 7,000 feet, and there is a continual vista of the snow ranges to the north and valleys and rivers to the south. Dhanaulti is one of the lovelier spots, and the Garhwal Mandal Vikas Nigam has a rest house here, where one can spend an idyllic weekend. Some years ago I walked all the way to Chamba, spending the night at Kaddukhal, from where a short climb takes one to the Surkhanda Devi temple.

Leaving the Tehri road, one can also trek down to the little Aglar river and then up to Nag Tibba, 9,000 feet, which has good oak forests and animals ranging from barking deer to Himalayan bear; but this is an arduous trek and you must be prepared to spend the night in the open or seek the hospitality of a village.

On this particular day, I reach Suakholi and rest in a tea shop, a loose stone structure with a tin roof held down by stones. It serves the bus passengers, mule drivers, milkmen and others who use this road.

I find a couple of mules tethered to a pine tree. The mule drivers, handsome men in tattered clothes, sit on a bench in the shade of the tree, drinking tea from brass tumblers. The shopkeeper, a man of indeterminate age—the cold dry winds from the mountain passes having crinkled his face like a walnut—greets me enthusiastically, as he always does. He even produces a chair, which looks a survivor from one of Wilson's rest houses, and may even be a Sheraton. Fortunately the Mussoorie kabaris do not know about it or they'd have snapped it up long ago. In any case, the stuffing has come out of the seat. The shopkeeper apologizes for its condition: 'The rats were nesting in it.' And then, to reassure me, he said: 'But they have gone now.'

I would just as soon be on the bench with the Jaunpuri mule drivers, but I do not wish to offend Mela Ram, the tea-shop owner; so I take his chair into the shade and lower myself into it.

'How long have you kept this shop?'

'Oh, ten, fifteen years, I do not remember.' He hasn't bothered to count the years. Why should he? Outside the towns in the isolation of the hills, life is simply a matter of yesterday, today and tomorrow. And not always tomorrow.

Unlike Mela Ram, the mule drivers have somewhere to go and something to deliver—sacks of potatoes! From Jaunpur to

Jaunsar, the potato is probably the crop best suited to these stony, terraced fields. They have to deliver their potatoes in the Landour bazaar and return to their village before nightfall; and soon they lead their pack animals away, along the dusty road to Mussoorie.

'Tea or lassi?' Mela Ram offers me a choice, and I choose the curd preparation, which is sharp, sour and very refreshing. The wind soughs gently in the upper branches of the pine trees, and I relax in my Sheraton chair like some eighteenth-century nawab who has brought his own furniture into the wilderness. I can see why Wilson did not want to return to the plains when he came this way in the 1850s. Instead he went further and higher into the mountains and made his home among the people of the Bhagirathi valley.

Having wandered some way down the Tehri road, it is quite late by the time I return to the Landour bazaar. Lights still twinkle on the hills, but shop fronts are shuttered and the little bazaar is silent. The people living on either side of the narrow street can hear my footsteps, and I hear their casual remarks, music, a burst of laughter.

Through a gap in the rows of buildings, I can see Pari Tibba outlined in the moonlight. A greenish phosphorescent glow appears to move here and there about the hillside. This is the 'fairy light' that gives the hill its name Pari Tibba, Fairy Hill. I have no explanation for it, and I don't know anyone else who has been able to explain it satisfactorily; but often from my window I see this greenish light zigzagging about the hill.

A three-quarter moon is up, and the tin roofs of the bazaar, drenched with dew, glisten in the moonlight. Although the street is unlit, I need no torch. I can see every step of the way. I can even read the headlines on the discarded newspaper lying in the gutter.

Although I am alone on the road, I am aware of the life, pulsating around me. It is a cold night, doors and windows are shut; but through the many clinks, narrow fingers of light reach out into the night. Who could still be up? A shopkeeper going through his accounts, a college student preparing for his exams, someone coughing and groaning in the dark.

Three stray dogs are romping in the middle of the road. It is their road now, and they abandon themselves to a wild chase, almost knocking me down.

A jackal slinks across the road, looking to the right and left—he knows his road-drill—to make sure the dogs have gone. A field rat wriggles through a hole in a rotting plank on its nightly foray among sacks of grain and pulses.

Yes, this is an old bazaar. The bakers, tailors, silversmiths and wholesale merchants are the grandsons of those who followed the mad sahibs to this hilltop in the thirties and forties of the last century. Most of them are plainsmen, quite prosperous, even though many of their houses are crooked and shaky.

Although the shopkeepers and tradesmen are fairly prosperous, the hill people—those who come from the surrounding Tehri and Jaunpur villages—are usually poor. Their small holdings and rocky fields do not provide them with much of a living, and men and boys have to often come into the hill station or go down to the cities in search of a livelihood. They pull rickshaws, or work in hotels and restaurants. Most of them have somewhere to stay.

But as I pass along the deserted street under the shadow of the clock tower, I find a boy huddled in a recess, a thin shawl wrapped around his shoulders. He is wide awake and shivering.

I pass by, my head down, my thoughts already on the warmth of my small cottage only a mile away. And then I stop.

It is almost as though the bright moonlight has stopped me, holding my shadow in thrall.

> If I am not for myself,
> Who will be for me?
> And if I am not for others,
> What am I?
> And if not now, when?

The words of an ancient sage beat upon my mind. I walk back to the shadows where the boy crouches. He does not say anything, but he looks up at me, puzzled and apprehensive. All the warnings of well-wishers crowd in upon me—stories of crime by night, of assault and robber, 'ill met by moonlight'.

But this is not northern Ireland or Lebanon or the streets of New York. This is Landour in the Garhwal Himalayas. And the boy is no criminal. I can tell from his features that he comes from the hills beyond Tehri. He has come here looking for work and has yet to find any.

'Have you somewhere to stay?' I ask.

He shakes his head; but something about my tone of voice has given him confidence, because now there is a glimmer of hope, a friendly appeal in his eyes.

I have committed myself. I cannot pass on. A shelter for the night—that's the very least one human should be able to expect from another.

'If you can walk some way,' I offer, 'I can give you a bed and blanket.'

He gets up immediately, a thin boy, wearing only a shirt and part of an old tracksuit. He follows me without any hesitation. I cannot now betray his trust. Nor can I fail to trust him.

FROM THE POOL TO THE GLACIER

My Boyhood Pool

It was going to rain. I could see the rain moving across the foothills, and I could smell it on the breeze. But instead of turning homewards I pushed my way through the leaves and brambles that grew across the forest path. I had heard the sound of running water at the bottom of the hill, and I was determined to find this hidden stream.

I had to slide down a rock-face into a small ravine and there I found the stream running over a bed of shingle, I removed my shoes and started walking upstream. A large, glossy black bird with a curved red beak hooted at me as I passed; and a paradise flycatcher—this one I couldn't fail to recognize, with its long fan-tail beating the air—swooped across the stream. Water trickled down from the hillside, from amongst ferns and grasses and wild flowers; and the hills, rising steeply on either side, kept the ravine in shadow. The rocks were smooth, almost soft, and some of them were grey and some yellow. A small waterfall came down the rocks and formed a deep, round pool of apple-green water.

When I saw the pool, I turned and ran home. I wanted to tell Anil and Kamal about it. It began to rain, but I didn't stop to take shelter, I ran all the way home—through the sal forest, across the dry riverbed through the outskirts of the town.

Though Anil usually chose the adventures we were to have, the pool was my own discovery, and I was proud of it. 'We'll call it Rusty's Pool,' said Kamal. 'And remember, it's a secret pool. No one else must know of it.'

I think it was the pool that brought us together more than anything else.

Kamal was the best swimmer. He dived off rocks and went gliding about under the water like a long golden fish. Anil had strong legs and arms, and he threshed about with much vigour but little skill. I could dive off a rock too, but I usually landed on my stomach.

There were slim silver fish in the stream. At first we tried catching them with a line, but they soon learnt the art of taking the bait without being caught on the hook. Next we tried a bedsheet (Anil had removed it from his mother's laundry) which we stretched across one end of the stream; but the fish wouldn't come anywhere near it. Eventually, Anil, without telling us, procured a stick of gunpowder. And Kamal and I were startled out of an afternoon siesta by a flash across the water and a deafening explosion. Half the hillside tumbled into the pool, and Anil along with it. We got him out, along with a large supply of stunned fish which were too small for eating. Anil, however, didn't want all his work to go to waste; so he roasted the fish over a fire and ate them himself.

The effects of the explosion gave Anil another idea, which was to enlarge our pool by building a dam across one end. This he accomplished with our combined labour. But he had chosen a week when there had been heavy rain in the hills, and we had barely finished the dam when a torrent of water came rushing down the bed of the stream and burst our earthworks, flooding the ravine. Our clothes were carried away by the current, and we had to wait until it was night before creeping into town through the darkest alleyways. Anil was spotted at a street corner, but he posed as a naked sadhu and began calling for alms, and finally slipped in through the back door of his house without being recognized. I had to lend Kamal some of my clothes, and these, being on the small side, made him look odd and gangly. Our other activities at the pool included wrestling and buffalo-riding.

We wrestled on a strip of sand that ran beside the stream. Anil had often attended wrestling akharas and was something of an expert. Kamal and I usually combined against him, and after five or ten minutes of furious, unscientific struggle, we usually succeeded in flattening Anil into the sand. Kamal would sit on his head, and I would sit on his legs, until he admitted defeat. There was no fun in taking him on singly, because he knew too many tricks for us.

We rode on a couple of buffaloes that sometimes came to drink and wallow in the more muddy parts of the stream. Buffaloes are fine, sluggish creatures, always in search of a soft, slushy resting place. We would climb on their backs, and kick and yell and urge them forward; but on no occasion did we succeed in getting them to carry us anywhere. If they tired of our antics, they would merely roll over on their backs, taking us with them into a bed of muddy water.

Not that it mattered how muddy we got, because we had only to dive into the pool to get rid of it all. The buffaloes couldn't get to the pool because of its narrow outlet and the slippery rocks.

If it was possible for Anil and me to leave our homes at night, we would come to the pool for a swim by moonlight. We would often find Kamal there before us. He wasn't afraid of the dark or the surrounding forest, where there were panthers and jungle cats. We bathed silently at nights, because the stillness of the surrounding jungle seemed to discourage high spirits; but sometimes Kamal would sing—he had a clear, ringing voice—and we would float the red, long-fingered poinsettias downstream.

The pool was to be our principal meeting place during the coming months. It was not that we couldn't meet in town. But the pool was secret, known only to us, and it gave us a feeling of conspiracy and adventure to meet there after school. It was at the pool that we made our plans: it was at the pool that we first spoke of the glacier; but several weeks and a few other exploits were to pass before the particular dream materialized.

Ghosts on the Veranda

Anil's mother's memory was stored with an incredible amount of folklore, and she would sometimes astonish us with her stories of spirits and mischievous ghosts.

One evening, when Anil's father was out of town, and Kamal and I had been invited to stay the night at Anil's upper-storey flat in the bazaar, his mother began to tell us about the various types of ghosts she had known. Mulia, a servant-girl, having just taken a bath, came out on the veranda with her hair loose.

'My girl, you ought not to leave your hair loose like that,' said Anil's mother. 'It is better to tie a knot in it.'

'But I have not oiled it yet,' said Mulia.

'Never mind, but you should not leave your hair loose

towards sunset. There are spirits called jinns who are attracted to long hair and pretty black eyes like yours. They may be tempted to carry you away!'

'How dreadful!' exclaimed Mulia, hurriedly tying a knot in her hair, and going indoors to be on the safe side. Kamal, Anil and I sat on a string cot, facing Anil's mother, who sat on another cot. She was not much older than thirty-two, and had often been mistaken for Anil's elder sister; she came from a village near Mathura, a part of the country famous for its gods and spirits, and demons.

'Can you see jinns, aunty-ji?' I asked.

'Sometimes,' she said. 'There was an Urdu teacher in Mathura, whose pupils were about the same age as you. One of the boys was very good at his lessons. One day, while he sat at his desk in a corner of the classroom, the teacher asked him to fetch a book from the cupboard which stood at the far end of the room. The boy, who felt lazy that morning, didn't move from his seat. He merely stretched out his hand, took the book from the cupboard, and handed it to the teacher. Everyone was astonished, because the boy's arm had stretched about four yards before touching the book! They realized that he was a jinn; that was the reason for his being so good at games and exercises which required great agility.'

'Well, I wish I was a jinn,' said Anil. 'Especially for volleyball matches.'

Anil's mother then told us about munjia, a mischievous ghost who lives in lonely peepul trees. When a munjia is annoyed, he rushes out from his tree and upsets tongas, bullock-carts and cycles. Even a bus is known to have been upset by a munjia.

'If you are passing beneath a peepul tree at night,' warned Anil's mother, 'be careful not to yawn without covering your mouth or snapping your fingers in front of it. If you don't remember to do that, the munjia will jump down your throat and completely ruin your digestion!'

In an attempt to change the subject, Kamal mentioned that a friend of his had found a snake in his bed one morning.

'Did he kill it?' asked Anil's mother anxiously.

'No, it slipped away,' said Kamal.

'Good,' she said. 'It is lucky if you see a snake early in the morning.'

'It won't bite you if you let it alone,' she said.

By eleven o'clock, after we had finished our dinner and heard a few more ghost stories—including one about Anil's grandmother, whose spirit paid the family a visit—Kamal and I were most reluctant to leave the company on the veranda and retire to the room which had been set apart for us. It did not make us feel any better to be told by Anil's mother that we should recite certain magical verses to keep away the more mischievous spirits. We tried one, which went—

Bhoot, pret, pisach, dana
Chhoo mantar, sab nikal jana,
Mano, mano, Shiv ka kahna...

which, roughly translated, means—

Ghosts, spirits, goblins, sprites,
Away you fly, don't come tonight,
Or with great Shiva you'll have to fight!

Shiva, the Destroyer, is one of the three major Hindu deities.

But the more we repeated the verse, the more uneasy we became, and when I got into bed (after carefully examining it for snakes), I couldn't lie still, but kept twisting and turning and looking at the walls for moving shadows. Kamal attempted to raise our spirits by singing softly, but this only made the atmosphere more eerie. After a while, we heard someone knocking at the door, and the voices of Anil and the maidservant. Getting up and opening the door, I found them looking pale and anxious. They, too, had succeeded in frightening themselves as a result of Anil's mother's stories.

'Are you all right?' asked Anil. 'Wouldn't you like to sleep in our part of the house? It might be safer. Mulia will help us carry the beds across!'

'We're quite all right,' protested Kamal and I, refusing to admit we were nervous; but we were hustled along to the other side of the flat as though a band of ghosts was conspiring against us. Anil's mother had been absent during all this activity but suddenly we heard her screaming from the direction of the room we had just left.

'Rusty and Kamal have disappeared!' she cried. 'Their beds have gone, too!'

And then, when she came out on the veranda and saw us dashing about in our pyjamas, she gave another scream and collapsed on a cot.

After that, we didn't allow Anil's mother to tell us ghost stories at night.

To the Hills

At the end of August, when the rains were nearly over, we met at the pool to make plans for the autumn holidays. We had bathed, and were stretched out in the shade of the fresh, rain-washed sal trees, when Kamal, pointing vaguely to the distant mountains, said: 'Why don't we go to the Pindari Glacier?'

'The glacier!' exclaimed Anil. 'But that's all snow and ice!'

'Of course it is,' said Kamal. 'But there's a path through the mountains that goes all the way to the foot of the glacier. It's only fifty-four miles!'

'Do you mean we must—*walk* fifty-four miles?'

'Well, there's no other way,' said Kamal. 'Unless you prefer to sit on a mule. But your legs are too long, they'll be trailing along the ground. No, we'll have to walk. It will take us about ten days to get to the glacier and back, but if we take enough food there'll be no problem. There are dak bungalows to stay in at night.'

'Kamal gets all the best ideas,' I said. 'But I suppose Anil and I will have to get our parents' permission. And some money.'

'My mother won't let me go,' said Anil. 'She says the mountains are full of ghosts. And she thinks I'll get up to some mischief. How can one get up to mischief on a lonely mountain?'

'I'm sure it won't be dangerous, people are always going to the glacier. Can you see that peak above the others on the right?' Kamal pointed to the distant snow-range, barely visible against the soft blue sky. 'The Pindari Glacier is below it. It's at 12,000 feet, I think, but we won't need any special equipment. There'll be snow only for the final two or three miles. Do you know that it's the beginning of the river Sarayu?'

'You mean our river?' asked Anil, thinking of the little river that wandered along the outskirts of the town, joining the Ganga further downstream.

'Yes. But it's only a trickle where it starts.'

'How much money will we need?' I asked, determined to be practical.

'Well, I've saved twenty rupees,' said Kamal.

'But won't you need that for your books?' I asked.

'No, this is extra. If each of us brings twenty rupees, we should have enough. There's nothing to spend money on, once we are up on the mountains. There are only one or two villages on the way, and food is scarce, so we'll have to take plenty of food with us. I learnt all this from the Tourist Office.'

'Kamal's been planning this without our knowledge,' complained Anil.

'He always plans in advance,' I said. 'But it's a good idea, and it should be a fine adventure.'

'All right,' said Anil. 'But Rusty will have to be with me when I ask my mother. She thinks Rusty is very sensible, and might let me go if he says it's quite safe.' And he ended the discussion by jumping into the pool, where we soon joined him.

Though my mother hesitated about letting me go, my father said it was a wonderful idea, and was only sorry because he couldn't accompany us himself (which was a relief, as we didn't want our parents along); and though Anil's father hesitated—or rather, because he hesitated—his mother said, yes, of course Anil must go, the mountain air would be good for his health. A puzzling remark, because Anil's health had never been better. The bazaar people, when they heard that Anil might be away for a couple of weeks, were overjoyed at the prospect of a quiet spell, and pressed his father to let him go.

On a cloudy day promising rain, we bundled ourselves into the bus that was to take us to Kapkote (where people lose their caps and coats, punned Anil), the starting point of our trek. Each of us carried a haversack, and we had also brought along a good-sized bedding roll which, apart from blankets, also contained rice and flour thoughtfully provided by Anil's mother. We had no idea how we would carry the bedding roll once we started walking; but an astrologer had told Anil's mother it was a good day for travelling, so we didn't worry much over minor details.

We were soon in the hills, on a winding road that took us up and up, until we saw the valley and our town spread out beneath us, the river a silver ribbon across the plain. Kamal pointed to a patch of dense sal forest and said, 'Our pool must be there!' We took a sharp bend, and the valley disappeared, and the mountains towered above us.

We had dull headaches by the time we reached Kapkote; but when we got down from the bus, a cool breeze freshened us. At the wayside shop, we drank glasses of hot, sweet tea, and the shopkeeper told us we could spend the night in one of his rooms. It was pleasant at Kapkote, the hills wooded with deodar trees, the lower slopes planted with fresh green paddy. At night, there was a wind moaning in the trees, and it found its way through the cracks in the windows and eventually through our blankets. Then, right outside the door, a dog began howling at the moon. It had been a good day for travelling, but the astrologer hadn't warned us that it would be a bad night for sleep.

Next morning, we washed our faces at a small stream about a hundred yards from the shop, and filled our water-bottles for the day's march. A boy from the nearby village sat on a rock, studying our movements.

'Where are you going?' he asked, unable to suppress his curiosity.

'To the glacier,' said Kamal.

'Let me come with you,' said the boy. 'I know the way.'

'You're too small,' said Anil. 'We need someone who can carry our bedding roll.'

'I'm small,' said the boy, 'but I'm strong. I'm not a weakling like the boys in the plains.' Though he was shorter than any of us, he certainly looked sturdy, and had a muscular, well-knit body and pink cheeks. 'See!' he said; and picking up a rock the size of a football, he heaved it across the stream.

'I think he can come with us,' I said.

And the boy, whose name was Bisnu, dashed off to inform his people of his employment—we had agreed to pay him a rupee a day for acting as our guide and 'sherpa'.

And then we were walking—at first, above the little Sarayu River, then climbing higher along the rough mule-track, always within sound of the water. Kamal wanted to bathe in the river. I said it was too far, and Anil said we wouldn't reach the dak bungalow before dark if we went for a swim. Regretfully, we left the river behind, and marched on through a forest of oaks, over wet, rotting leaves that made a soft carpet for our feet. We ate at noon, under an oak. As we didn't want to waste any time making a fire—not on this first crucial day—we ate beans from a tin and drank most of our water.

In the afternoon, we came to the river again. The water was swifter now, green and bubbling, still far below us. We saw two boys in the water, swimming in an inlet which reminded us of our own secret pool. They waved, and invited us to join them. We returned their greeting; but it would have taken us an hour to get down to the river and up again; so we continued on our way.

We walked fifteen miles on the first day—our speed was to decrease after this—and we were at the dak bungalow by six o'clock. Bisnu busied himself collecting sticks for a fire. Anil found the bungalow's watchman asleep in a patch of fading sunlight, and roused him. The watchman, who hadn't been bothered by visitors for weeks, grumbled at our intrusion, and opened a room for us. He also produced some potatoes from his quarters, and these were roasted for dinner.

It became cold after the sun had gone down, and we remained close to Bisnu's fire. The damp sticks burnt fitfully. But Bisnu had justified his inclusion in our party. He had balanced the bedding roll on his shoulders as though it were full of cotton wool instead of blankets. Now he was helping with the cooking. And we were glad to have him sharing our hot potatoes and strong tea.

There were only two beds in the room, and we pushed these together, apportioning out the blankets as fairly as possible. Then the four of us leapt into bed, shivering in the cold. We were already over 5,000 feet. Bisnu, in his own peculiar way, had wrapped a scarf around his neck, though a cotton singlet and shorts were all that he wore for the night.

'Tell us a story, Rusty,' said Anil. 'It will help us fall asleep.'

I told them one of his mother's stories, about a boy and a girl who had been changed into a pair of buffaloes; and then Bisnu told us about the ghost of a sadhu, who was to be seen sitting in the snow by moonlight, not far from the glacier. Far from putting us to sleep, this story kept us awake for hours.

'Aren't you asleep yet?' I asked Anil in the middle of the night.

'No, you keep kicking me,' he lied.

'We don't have enough blankets,' complained Kamal, 'it's too cold to sleep.'

'I never sleep till it's very late,' mumbled Bisnu from the bottom of the bed.

No one was prepared to admit that our imaginations were keeping us awake.

After a little while we heard a thud on the corrugated tin sheeting, and then the sound of someone—or something—

scrambling about on the roof. Anil, Kamal and I sat up in bed, startled out of our wits. Bisnu, who had been winning the race to be fast asleep, merely turned over on his side and grunted.

'It's only a bear,' he said. 'Didn't you notice the pumpkins on the roof? Bears love pumpkins.'

For half an hour, we had to listen to the bear as it clambered about on the roof, feasting on the watchman's ripening pumpkins. Finally, there was silence. Kamal and I crawled out of our blankets and went to the window. And through the frosted glass we saw a Himalayan black bear ambling across the slope in front of the bungalow, a fat pumpkin held between its paws.

To the River

It was raining when we woke, and the mountains were obscured by a heavy mist. We delayed our departure, playing football on the veranda with one of the pumpkins that had fallen off the roof. At noon, the rain stopped, and the sun shone through the clouds. As the mist lifted, we saw the snow range, the great peaks of Nanda Kot and Trisul stepping into the sky.

'It's different up here,' said Kamal. 'I feel like a different person.'

'That's the altitude,' I said. 'As we go higher, we'll get lighter in the head.'

'Anil is light in the head already,' said Kamal. 'I hope the altitude isn't too much for him.'

'If you two are going to be witty,' said Anil, 'I shall go off with Bisnu, and you'll have to find the way yourselves.'

Bisnu grinned at each of us in turn to show us that he wasn't taking sides; and after a breakfast of boiled eggs, we set off on our trek to the next bungalow.

Rain had made the ground slippery, and we were soon ankle-deep in slush. Our next bungalow lay in a narrow valley, on the banks of the rushing Pindar River, which twisted its way through the mountains. We were not sure how far we had to go, but nobody seemed in a hurry. On an impulse, I decided to hurry on ahead of the others. I wanted to be waiting for them at the river.

The path dropped steeply, then rose and went round a big mountain. I met a woodcutter and asked him how far it was to the river. He was a short, stocky man, with gnarled hands and a weathered face.

'Seven miles,' he said. 'Are you alone?'

'No, the others are following, but I cannot wait for them. If you meet them, tell them I'll be waiting at the river.'

The path descended steeply now, and I had to run a little. It was a dizzy, winding path. The hillside was covered with lush green ferns and, in the trees, unseen birds sang loudly. Soon, I was in the valley, and the path straightened out. A girl was coming from the opposite direction. She held a long, curved knife, with which she had been cutting grass and fodder. There were rings in her nose and ears, and her arms were covered with heavy bangles. The bangles made music when she moved her hands—it was as though her hands spoke a language of their own.

'How far is it to the river?' I asked.

The girl had probably never been near the river, or she may have been thinking of another one, because she replied, 'Twenty miles,' without any hesitation.

I laughed, and ran down the path. A parrot screeched suddenly, flew low over my head—a flash of blue and green—and took the course of the path, while I followed its dipping flight, until the path rose and the bird disappeared into the trees.

A trickle of water came from the hillside, and I stopped to drink. The water was cold and sharp and very refreshing. I had walked alone for nearly an hour. Presently I saw a boy ahead of me, driving a few goats along the path.

'How far is it to the river?' I asked, when I caught up with him.

The boy said, 'Oh, not far, just around the next hill.'

As I was hungry, I produced some dry bread from my pocket and, breaking it in two, offered half to the boy. We sat on the grassy hillside and ate in silence. Then we walked on together and began talking; and I did not notice the smarting of my feet and the distance I had covered. But after some time the boy had to diverge along another path, and I was once more on my own.

I missed the village boy. I looked up and down the path, but I could see no one, no sign of Anil and Kamal and Bisnu, and the river was not in sight either. I began to feel discouraged. But I couldn't turn back; I was determined to be at the river before the others.

And so I walked on, along the muddy path, past terraced fields and small stone houses, until there were no more fields and houses, only forest and sun and silence.

The silence was oppressive and a little frightening. It was different from the silence of a room or an empty street. Nor was there any movement, except for the bending of grass beneath my feet, and the circling of a hawk high above the fir trees.

And then, as I rounded a sharp bend, the silence broke into sound.

The sound of the river.

Far down in the valley, the river tumbled over itself in its impatience to reach the plains. I began to run, slipped and stumbled, but continued running.

And the water was blue and white and wonderful.

When Anil, Kamal and Bisnu arrived, the four of us bravely decided to bathe in the little river. The late afternoon sun was still warm, but the water—so clear and inviting—proved to be ice-cold. Only twenty miles upstream the river emerged as a little trickle from the glacier, and in its swift descent down the mountain slopes it did not give the sun a chance to penetrate its waters. But we were determined to bathe, to wash away the dust and sweat of our two days' trudging, and we leapt about in the shallows like startled porpoises, slapping water on each other, and gasping with the shock of each immersion. Bisnu, more accustomed to mountain streams than ourselves, ventured across in an attempt to catch an otter but wasn't fast enough. Then we were on the springy grass, wrestling each other in order to get warm.

The bungalow stood on a ledge just above the river, and the sound of the water rushing down the mountain defile could be heard at all times. The sound of the birds, which we had grown used to, was drowned by the sound of the water; but the birds themselves could be seen, many-coloured, standing out splendidly against the dark green forest foliage: the red-crowned jay, the paradise flycatcher, the purple whistling-thrush, others we could not recognize.

Higher up the mountain, above some terraced land where oats and barley were grown, stood a small cluster of huts. This, we were told by the watchman, was the last village on the way to the glacier. It was, in fact, one of the last villages in India, because if we crossed the difficult passes beyond the glacier, we would find ourselves in Tibet. We told the watchman we would be quite satisfied if we reached the glacier.

Then Anil made the mistake of mentioning the Abominable Snowman, of whom we had been reading in the papers. The people of Nepal believe in the existence of the Snowman, and our watchman was a Nepali.

'Yes, I have seen the Yeti,' he told us. 'A great shaggy flat-footed creature. In the winter, when it snows heavily, he passes by the bungalow at night. I have seen his tracks the next morning.'

'Does he come this way in the summer?' I asked anxiously. We were sitting before another of Bisnu's fires, drinking tea with condensed milk, and trying to get through a black, sticky sweet which the watchman had produced from his tin trunk.

'The Yeti doesn't come here in the summer,' said the old man. 'But I have seen the Lidini sometimes. You have to be careful of her.'

'What is a Lidini?' asked Kamal.

'Ah!' said the watchman mysteriously. 'You have heard of the Abominable Snowman, no doubt, but there are few who have heard of the Abominable Snowwoman! And yet she is by far the more dangerous of the two!'

'What is she like?' asked Anil, and we all craned forward.

'She is of the same height as the Yeti—about seven feet when her back is straight—and her hair is much longer. She has very long teeth and nails. Her feet face inwards, but she can run very fast, especially downhill. If you see a Lidini, and she chases you, always run away in an uphill direction. She tires quickly because of her feet. But when running downhill she has no trouble at all, and you have to be very fast to escape her!'

'Well, we're all good runners,' said Anil with a nervous laugh, 'but it's just a fairy story, I don't believe a word of it.'

'But you *must* believe fairy stories,' I said, remembering a performance of Peter Pan in London, when those in the audience who believed in fairies were asked to clap their hands in order to save Tinker Bell's life. 'Even if they aren't true,' I added, deciding there was a world of difference between Tinker Bell and the Abominable Snowwoman.

'Well, I don't believe there's a Snowman or a Snow-woman!' declared Anil.

The watchman was most offended and refused to tell us anything about the Sagpa and Sagpani; but Bisnu knew about them, and later, when we were in bed, he told us that they were similar to Snowmen but much smaller. Their favourite pastime was sleeping, and they became very annoyed if anyone woke them, and became ferocious, and did not give one much time to start running uphill. The Sagpa and Sagpani sometimes kidnapped small children, and taking them to their cave, would look after the children very carefully, feeding them on fruits, honey, rice, and earthworms.

'When the Sagpa isn't looking,' he said, 'you can throw the earthworms over your shoulder.'

The Glacier

It was a fine sunny morning when we set out to cover the last seven miles to the glacier. We had expected this to be a stiff climb, but the last dak bungalow was situated at well over 10,000 feet above sea level, and the ascent was to be fairly gradual.

And suddenly, abruptly, there were no more trees. As the bungalow dropped out of sight, the trees and bushes gave way to short grass and little blue and pink alpine flowers. The snow peaks were close now, ringing us in on every side. We passed waterfalls, cascading hundreds of feet down precipitous rock faces, thundering into the little river. A great golden eagle hovered over us for some time.

'I feel different again,' said Kamal.

'We're very high now,' I said. 'I hope we won't get headaches.'

'I've got one already,' complained Anil. 'Let's have some tea.'

We had left our cooking utensils at the bungalow, expecting to return there for the night, and had brought with us only a few biscuits, chocolate and a thermos of tea. We finished the tea, and Bisnu scrambled about on the grassy slopes, collecting wild strawberries. They were tiny strawberries, very sweet, and they did nothing to satisfy our appetites. There was no sign of habitation or human life.

The only creatures to be found at that height were the gorals—sure-footed mountain goats—and an occasional snow leopard, or a bear.

We found and explored a small cave, and then, turning a bend, came unexpectedly upon the glacier.

The hill fell away, and there, confronting us, was a great white field of snow and ice, cradled between two peaks that could only have been the abode of the gods. We were speechless for several minutes. Kamal took my hand and held on to it for reassurance; perhaps he was not sure that what he saw was real. Anil's mouth hung open. Bisnu's eyes glittered with excitement.

We proceeded cautiously on the snow, supporting each other on the slippery surface; but we could not go far, because we were quite unequipped for any high-altitude climbing. It was pleasant to feel that we were the only boys in our town who had climbed so high. A few black rocks jutted out from the snow, and we sat down on them, to feast our eyes on the view. The sun reflected sharply from the snow, and we felt surprisingly warm.

'Let's sunbathe!' said Anil, on a sudden impulse.

'Yes, let's do that!' I said.

In a few minutes, we had taken off our clothes and, sitting on the rocks, were exposing ourselves to the elements. It was delicious to feel the sun crawling over my skin. Within half an hour I was post-box red, and so was Bisnu, and the two of us decided to get into our clothes before the sun scorched the skin off our backs. Kamal and Anil appeared to be more resilient to sunlight, and laughed at our discomfiture. Bisnu and I avenged ourselves by gathering up handfuls of snow and rubbing it on their backs. We dressed quickly enough after that, Anil leaping about like a performing monkey.

Meanwhile, almost imperceptibly, clouds had covered some of the peaks, and white mist drifted down the mountain slopes. It was time to get back to the bungalow; we would barely make it before dark.

We had not gone far when lightning began to sizzle about the mountaintops followed by waves of thunder.

'Let's run!' shouted Anil. 'We can get shelter in the cave!'

The clouds could hold themselves in no longer, and the rain came down suddenly, stinging our faces as it was whipped up by an icy wind. Half-blinded, we ran as fast as we could along the slippery path, and stumbled, drenched and exhausted, into the little cave.

The cave was mercifully dry, and not very dark. We remained at the entrance, watching the rain sweep past us, listening to the wind whistling down the long gorge.

'It will take some time to stop,' said Kamal.

'No, it will pass soon,' said Bisnu. 'These storms are short and fierce.'

Anil produced his pocketknife, and to pass the time we carved our names in the smooth rock of the cave.

'We will come here again, when we are older,' said Kamal, 'and perhaps our names will still be here.'

It had grown dark by the time the rain stopped. A full moon helped us find our way, we went slowly and carefully. The rain had loosened the earth, and stones kept rolling down the hillside. I was afraid of starting a landslide.

'I hope we don't meet the Lidini now,' said Anil fervently.

'I thought you didn't believe in her,' I said.

'I don't,' replied Anil. 'But what if I'm wrong?'

We saw only a mountain goat, the goral, poised on the brow of a precipice, silhouetted against the sky.

And then the path vanished.

Had it not been for the bright moonlight, we might have walked straight into an empty void. The rain had caused a landslide, and where there had been a narrow path there was now only a precipice of loose, slippery shale.

'We'll have to go back,' said Bisnu. 'It will be too dangerous to try and cross in the dark.'

'We'll sleep in the cave,' I suggested.

'We've nothing to sleep in,' said Anil. 'Not a single blanket between us and nothing to eat!'

'We'll just have to rough it till morning,' said Kamal. 'It will be better than breaking our necks here.'

We returned to the cave, which did at least have the virtue of being dry. Bisnu had matches, and he made a fire with some dry sticks which had been left in the cave by a previous party. We ate what was left of a loaf of bread.

There was no sleep for any of us that night. We lay close to each other for comfort, but the ground was hard and uneven. And every noise we heard outside the cave made us think of leopards and bears and even the Abominable Snowmen.

We got up as soon as there was a faint glow in the sky. The snow peaks were bright pink, but we were too tired and hungry and worried to care for the beauty of the sunrise. We took the path to the landslide, and once again looked for a way across. Kamal ventured to take a few steps on the loose pebbles, but the ground gave way immediately, and we had to grab him by the arms and shoulders to prevent him from sliding a hundred feet down the gorge.

'Now what are we going to do?' I asked.

'Look for another way,' said Bisnu.

'But do you know of any?'

And we all turned to look at Bisnu, expecting him to provide the solution to our problem.

'I have heard of a way,' said Bisnu, 'but I have never used it. It will be a little dangerous, I think. The path has not been used for several years—not since the traders stopped coming in from Tibet.'

'Never mind, we'll try it,' said Anil.

'We will have to cross the glacier first,' said Bisnu. 'That's the main problem.'

We looked at each other in silence. The glacier didn't look difficult to cross, but we know that it would not be easy for novices. For almost two furlongs it consisted of hard, slippery ice.

Anil was the first to arrive at a decision.

'Come on,' he said. 'There's no time to waste.'

We were soon on the glacier. And we remained on it for a long time. For every two steps forward, we slid one step backward. Our progress was slow and awkward. Sometimes, after advancing several yards across the ice at a steep incline, one of us would slip back and the others would have to slither down to help him up. At one particularly difficult spot, I dropped our water bottle and, grabbing at it, lost my footing, fell full-length and went sliding some twenty feet down the ice slope.

I had sprained my wrist and hurt my knee, and was to prove a liability for the rest of the trek.

Kamal tied his handkerchief around my hand, and Anil took charge of the water bottle, which we had filled with ice. Using my good hand to grab Bisnu's legs whenever I slipped, I struggled on behind the others.

It was almost noon, and we were quite famished, when we put our feet on grass again. And then we had another steep climb, clutching at roots and grasses, before we reached the path that Bisnu had spoken about. It was little more than a goat-track, but it took us around the mountain and brought us within sight of the dak bungalow.

'I could eat a whole chicken,' said Kamal.

'I could eat two,' I said.

'I could eat a Snowman,' said Bisnu.

'And I could eat the chowkidar,' said Anil.

Fortunately for the chowkidar, he had anticipated our hunger; and when we staggered into the bungalow late in the afternoon, we found a meal waiting for us. True, there was no chicken—but, so ravenous did we feel, that even the lowly onion tasted delicious!

We had Bisnu to thank for getting us back successfully. He had brought us over mountain and glacier with all the skill and confidence of a boy who had the Himalaya in his blood.

We took our time getting back to Kapkote; fished in the Sarayu River; bathed with the village boys we had seen on our way up; collected strawberries and ferns and wild flowers; and finally said goodbye to Bisnu.

Anil wanted to take Bisnu along with us, but the boy's

parents refused to let him go, saying that he was too young for the life of a city; but we were of the opinion that Bisnu could have taught the city boys a few things.

'Never mind,' said Kamal. 'We'll go on another trip next year, and we'll take you with us, Bisnu. We'll write and let you know our plans.'

This promise made Bisnu happy, and he saw us off at the bus stop, shouldering our bedding to the end. Then he skimmed up the trunk of a fir tree to have a better view of us leaving, and we saw him waving to us from the tree as our bus went round the bend from Kapkote, and the hills were left behind and the plains stretched out below.

HOW FAR IS THE RIVER?

Between the boy and the river was a mountain. I was a small boy, and it was a small river, but the mountain was big.

The thickly forested mountain hid the river, but I knew it was there and what it looked like. I had never seen the river with my own eyes, but from the villagers I had heard of it, of the fish in its waters, of its rocks and currents and waterfalls, and it only remained for me to touch the water and know it personally.

I stood in front of our house on the hill opposite the mountain, and gazed across the valley, dreaming of the river. I was barefooted; not because I couldn't afford shoes, but because I felt free with my feet bare—because I liked the feel of warm stones and cool grass, because not wearing shoes saved me the trouble of taking them off.

It was eleven o'clock and I knew my parents wouldn't be home till evening. There was a loaf of bread I could take with me, and on the way I might find some fruit. Here was the chance I had been waiting for; it would not come again for a long time, because it was seldom that my father and mother visited friends for the entire day. If I came back before dark, they wouldn't know where I had been.

I went into the house and wrapped the loaf of bread in a newspaper. Then I closed all the doors and windows.

The path to the river dropped steeply into the valley, then rose and went round the big mountain. It was frequently used by the villagers, woodcutters, milkmen, shepherds, mule drivers—but there were no villages beyond the mountain or near the river.

I passed a woodcutter and asked him how far it was to the river. He was a short, powerful man, with a creased and weathered face, and muscles that stood out in hard lumps.

'Seven miles,' he said. 'Why do you want to know?'

'I am going there,' I said.

'Alone?'

'Of course.'

'It will take you three hours to reach it, and then you have to come back. It will be getting dark, and it is not an easy road.'

'But I'm a good walker,' I said, though I had never walked further than the two miles between our house and my school. I left the woodcutter on the path, and continued down the hill.

It was a dizzy, winding path, and I slipped once or twice and slid into a bush or down a slope of slippery pine needles. The hill was covered with lush green ferns, the trees were entangled in creepers and a great wild dahlia would suddenly rear its golden head from the leaves and ferns.

Soon, I was in the valley, and the path straightened out and then began to rise. I met a girl who was coming from the opposite direction. She held a long curved knife with which she had been cutting grass, and there were rings in her nose and ears and her arms were covered with heavy bangles. The bangles made music when she moved her wrists. It was as though her hands spoke a language of their own.

'How far is it to the river?' I asked.

The girl had probably never been to the river, or she may have been thinking of another one, because she said, 'Twenty miles,' without any hesitation.

I laughed and ran down the path. A parrot screeched suddenly, flew low over my head, a flash of blue and green. It took the course of the path, and I followed its dipping flight, running until the path rose and the bird disappeared amongst the trees.

A trickle of water came down the hillside, and I stopped to drink. The water was cold and sharp but very refreshing. But I was soon thirsty again. The sun was striking the side of the hill, and the dusty path became hotter, the stones scorching my feet. I was sure I had covered half the distance: I had been walking for over an hour.

Presently, I saw another boy ahead of me driving a few goats down the path.

'How far is the river?' I asked.

The village boy smiled and said, 'Oh, not far, just round the next hill and straight down.'

Feeling hungry, I unwrapped my loaf of bread and broke it in two, offering one half to the boy. We sat on the hillside and ate in silence.

When we had finished, we walked on together and began talking; and talking I did not notice the smarting of my feet and the heat of the sun, the distance I had covered and the distance I had yet to cover. But after some time my companion had to take another path, and once more I was on my own.

I missed the village boy; I looked up and down the mountain path but no one else was in sight. My own home was hidden from view by the side of the mountain, and there was no sign of the river. I began to feel discouraged. If someone had been with me, I would not have faltered; but alone, I was conscious of my fatigue and isolation.

But I had come more than half way, and I couldn't turn back; I had to see the river. If I failed, I would always be a little ashamed of the experience. So I walked on, along the hot, dusty, stony path, past stone huts and terraced fields, until there were no more fields or huts, only forest and sun and loneliness. There were no men, and no sign of man's influence—only trees and rocks and grass and small flowers and silence...

The silence was impressive and a little frightening. There was no movement, except for the bending of grass beneath my feet, and the circling of a hawk against the blind blue of the sky.

Then, as I rounded a sharp bend, I heard the sound of water. I gasped with surprise and happiness, and began to run. I slipped and stumbled, but I kept on running, until I was able to plunge into the snow-cold mountain water.

And the water was blue and white and wonderful.

A NIGHT WALK HOME

No night is so dark as it seems.

Here in Landour, on the first range of the Himalayas, I have grown accustomed to the night's brightness—moonlight, starlight, lamplight, firelight! Even fireflies light up the darkness.

Over the years, the night has become my friend. On the one hand, it gives me privacy; on the other, it provides me with limitless freedom.

Not many people relish the dark. There are some who will even sleep with their lights burning all night. They feel safer that way. Safer from the phantoms conjured up by their imaginations. A primeval instinct, perhaps, going back to the time when primitive man hunted by day and was in turn hunted by night.

And yet, I have always felt safer by night, provided I do not deliberately wander about on clifftops or roads where danger is known to lurk. It's true that burglars and lawbreakers often work by night, their principal object being to get into other people's houses and make off with the silver or the family jewels. They are not into communing with the stars. Nor are late-night revellers, who are usually to be found in brightly lit places and are thus easily avoided. The odd drunk stumbling home is quite harmless and probably in need of guidance.

I feel safer by night, yes, but then I do have the advantage of living in the mountains, in a region where crime and random violence are comparatively rare. I know that if I were living in a big city in some other part of the world, I would think twice about walking home at midnight, no matter how pleasing the night sky would be.

Walking home at midnight in Landour can be quite eventful, but in a different sort of way. One is conscious all the time of the silent life in the surrounding trees and bushes. I have smelt a leopard without seeing it. I have seen jackals on the prowl. I have watched foxes dance in the moonlight. I have seen flying squirrels flit from one treetop to another. I have observed pine martens on their nocturnal journeys, and listened to the calls of nightjars and owls and other birds who live by night. Not all on the same night, of course. That would be a case of too many riches all at once. Some night walks can be uneventful. But usually there is something to see or hear or sense. Like those foxes dancing in the moonlight. One night, when I got home, I sat down and wrote these lines:

> As I walked home last night,
> I saw a lone fox dancing
> In the bright moonlight.
> I stood and watched; then
> Took the low road, knowing
> The night was his by right.
> Sometimes, when words ring true,
> I'm like a lone fox dancing
> In the morning dew.

Who else, apart from foxes, flying squirrels and night-loving writers are at home in the dark? Well, there are the nightjars, not much to look at, although their large, lustrous eyes gleam uncannily in the light of a lamp. But their sounds are distinctive. The breeding call of the Indian nightjar resembles the sound of a stone skimming over the surface of a frozen pond; it can be heard for a considerable distance. Another species utters a loud grating call which, when close at hand, sounds exactly like a whiplash cutting the air. 'Horsfield's nightjar' (with which I am more familiar in Mussoorie) makes a noise similar to that made by striking a plank with a hammer.

I must not forget the owls, those most celebrated of night birds, much maligned by those who fear the night. Most owls have very pleasant calls. The little jungle owlet has a note which is both mellow and musical. One misguided writer has likened its call to a motorcycle starting up, but this is libel. If only motorcycles sounded like the jungle owl, the world would be a more peaceful place to live and sleep in.

Then there is the little scops owl, who speaks only in monosyllables, occasionally saying 'wow' softly but with great deliberation. He will continue to say 'wow' at intervals of about a minute, for several hours throughout the night.

Probably the most familiar of Indian owls is the spotted owlet, a noisy bird who pours forth a volley of chuckles and squeaks in the early evening and at intervals all night. Towards sunset, I watch the owlets emerge from their holes one after another. Before coming out, each puts out a queer little round head with staring eyes. After they have emerged, they usually sit very quietly for a time as though only half awake. Then, all of a sudden, they begin to chuckle, finally breaking out in a torrent of chattering. Having in this way 'psyched' themselves into the right frame of mind, they spread their short, rounded wings and sail off for the night's hunting.

And I wend my way homewards. 'Night with her train of stars' is always enticing. The poet Henley found her so. But he also wrote of 'her great gift of sleep', and it is this gift that I am now about to accept with gratitude and humility.

A VILLAGE IN GARHWAL

I wake to what sounds like the din of a factory buzzer, but is in fact the music of a single vociferous cicada in the lime tree near my window.

Through the open window, I focus on a pattern of small, glossy lime leaves; then through them I see the mountains, the Himalayas, striding away into an immensity of sky.

'In a thousand ages of the gods I could not tell thee of the glories of Himachal.' So confessed a Sanskrit poet at the dawn of Indian history and he came closer than anyone else to capturing the spell of the Himalayas. The sea has had Conrad and Stevenson and Masefield, but the mountains continue to defy the written word. We have climbed their highest peaks and crossed their most difficult passes, but still they keep their secrets and their reserve; they remain remote, mysterious, spirit-haunted.

No wonder then, that the people who live on the mountain slopes in the mist-filled valleys of Garhwal have long since learned humility, patience and a quiet resignation. Deep in the crouching mist lie their villages, while climbing the mountain slopes are forests of rhododendron, spruce and deodar, soughing in the wind from the ice-bound passes. Pale women plough, they laugh at the thunder as their men go down to the plains for work;

for little grows on the beautiful mountains in the north wind.

When I think of Manjari village in Garhwal, I see a small river, a tributary of the Ganga, rushing along the bottom of a steep, rocky valley. On the banks of the river and on the terraced hills above, there are small fields of corn, barley, mustard, potatoes and onions. A few fruit trees grow near the village. Some hillsides are rugged and bare, just masses of quartz or granite. On hills exposed to wind, only grass and small shrubs are able to obtain a foothold.

This landscape is typical of Garhwal, one of India's most northerly regions with its massive snow ranges bordering on Tibet. Although thinly populated, it does not provide much of a living for its people. Most Garhwali cultivators are poor, some are very poor. 'You have beautiful scenery,' I observed after crossing the first range of hills.

'Yes,' said my friend, 'but we cannot eat the scenery.'

And yet these are cheerful people, sturdy and with wonderful powers of endurance. Somehow they manage to wrest a precarious living from the unhelpful, calcinated soil. I am their guest for a few days.

My friend Gajadhar has brought me to his home, to his village above the little Nayar River. We took a train into the foothills and then we took a bus and finally, made dizzy by the hairpin bends devised in the last century by a brilliantly diabolical road-engineer, we alighted at the small hill station of Lansdowne, chief recruiting centre for the Garhwal Regiment.

Lansdowne is just over 6,000 feet high. From there we walked, covering twenty-five miles between sunrise and sunset, until we came to Manjari village, clinging to the terraced slopes of a very proud, very permanent mountain.

And this is my fourth morning in the village.

Other mornings I was woken by the throaty chuckles of the red-billed blue magpies, as they glided between oak trees and medlars; but today the cicada has drowned all birdsong. It is a little out of season for cicadas but perhaps this sudden warm spell in late September has deceived him into thinking it is mating season again.

Early though it is, I am the last to get up. Gajadhar is exercising in the courtyard, going through an odd combination of Swedish exercises and yoga. He has a fine physique with the sturdy legs that most Garhwalis possess. I am sure he will realize his ambition of joining the Indian army as a cadet. His younger brother Chakradhar, who is slim and fair with high cheekbones, is milking the family's buffalo. Normally, he would be on his long walk to school, five miles distant; but this is a holiday, so he can stay at home and help with the household chores.

His mother is lighting a fire. She is a handsome woman, even though her ears, weighed down by heavy silver earrings, have lost their natural shape. Garhwali women usually invest their savings in silver ornaments. And at the time of marriage, it is the boy's parents who make a gift of land to the parents of an attractive girl; a dowry system in reverse. There are fewer women than men in the hills and their good looks and sturdy physique give them considerable status among the menfolk.

Chakradhar's father is a corporal in the Indian army and is away for most of the year.

When Gajadhar marries, his wife will stay in the village to help his mother and younger brother look after the fields, house, goats and buffalo. Gajadhar will see her only when he comes home on leave. He prefers it that way; he does not think a simple hill girl should be exposed to the sophisticated temptations of the plains.

The village is far above the river and most of the fields depend on rainfall. But water must be fetched for cooking, washing and drinking. And so, after a breakfast of hot sweet milk and thick chapattis stuffed with minced radish, the brothers and I set off down the rough track to the river.

The sun has climbed the mountains, but it has yet to reach the narrow valley. We bathe in the river. Gajadhar and Chakradhar dive off a massive rock; but I wade in circumspectly, unfamiliar with the river's depths and currents. The water, a milky blue, has come from the melting snows; it is very cold. I bathe quickly and then dash for a strip of sand where a little sunshine has split down the mountainside in warm, golden pools of light. At the same time, the song of the whistling thrush emerges like a dark secret from the wooded shadows.

A little later, buckets filled we toil up the steep mountain. We must go by a better path this time if we are not to come tumbling down with our buckets of water. As we climb, we are mocked by a barbet which sits high up in a spruce calling feverishly in its monotonous mournful way.

'We call it the mewli bird,' says Gajadhar. 'There is a story about it. People say that the souls of men who have suffered injuries in the law courts of the plains and who have died of their disappointments, transmigrate into the mewli birds. That is why the birds are always crying *un-nee-ow, un-nee-ow*, which means "injustice, injustice!"'

The path leads us past a primary school, a small temple and a single shop in which it is possible to buy salt, soap and a few other necessities. It is also the post office. And today it is serving as a lock-up.

The villagers have apprehended a local thief, who specializes in stealing jewellery from women while they are working in the fields. He is awaiting escort to the Lansdowne police station, and the shop-keeper-cum-postmaster-cum-constable brings him out for us to inspect. He is a mild-looking fellow, clearly shy of the small crowd that has gathered round him. I wonder how he manages to deprive the strong hill-women of their jewellery; it could not be by force! In any case, crimes of violence are rare in Garhwal; and robbery too, is uncommon for the simple reason that there is very little to rob.

The thief is rather glad of my presence, as it distracts attention from him. Strangers seldom come to Manjari. The crowd leaves him, turns to me, eager to catch a glimpse of the stranger in its midst. The children exclaim, point at me with delight, chatter among themselves. I might be a visitor from another planet instead of just an itinerant writer from the plains.

The postman has yet to arrive. The mail is brought in relays from Lansdowne. The Manjari postman who has to cover eight miles and delivers letters at several small villages on his route, should arrive around noon. He also serves as a newspaper, bringing the villagers news of the outside world. Over the years, he has acquired a reputation for being highly inventive, sometimes creating his own news, so much so that when he told the villagers that men had landed on the moon, no one believed him. There are still a few sceptics.

Gajadhar has been walking out of the village every day, anxious to meet the postman. He is expecting a letter giving the results of his army entrance examination. If he is successful he will be called for an interview. And then, if he is accepted, he will be trained as an officer-cadet. After two years he will become a second lieutenant. His father, after twelve years in the army, is still only a corporal. But his father never went to school. There were no schools in the hills during the father's youth.

The Manjari school is only up to Class 5 and it has about forty pupils. If these children (most of them boys) want to study any further, then, like Chakradhar, they must walk the five miles to the high school in the next big village.

'Don't you get tired walking ten miles every day?' I ask Chakradhar.

'I am used to it,' he says. 'I like walking.'

I know that he only has two meals a day—one at seven in the morning when he leaves home and the other at six or seven in the evening when he returns from school—and I ask him if he does not get hungry on the way.

'There is always the wild fruit,' he replies.

It appears that he is an expert on wild fruit: the purple berries of the thorny bilberry bushes ripening in May and June; wild strawberries like drops of blood on the dark green monsoon grass; small sour cherries and tough medlars in the winter months. Chakradhar's strong teeth and probing tongue extract whatever tang or sweetness lies hidden in them. And in March, there are the rhododendron flowers. His mother makes them into jam. But Chakradhar likes them as they are: he places the petals on his tongue and chews till the sweet juice trickles down his throat.

He has never been ill.

'But what happens when someone is ill?' I ask, knowing that in Manjari there are no medicines, no dispensary or hospital.

'He goes to bed until he is better,' says Gajadhar. 'We have a few home remedies. But if someone is very sick, we carry the person to the hospital at Lansdowne.' He pauses as though wondering how much he should say, then shrugs and says: 'Last year my uncle was very ill. He had a terrible pain in his stomach. For two days he cried out with the pain. So we made a litter and started out for Lansdowne. We had already carried him fifteen miles when he died. And then we had to carry him back again.'

Some of the villages have dispensaries managed by compounders but the remoter areas of Garhwal are completely without medical aid. To the outsider, life in the Garhwal hills may seem idyllic and the people simple. But the Garhwali is far from being simple and his life is one long struggle, especially if he happens to be living in a high altitude village snowbound for four months in the year, with cultivation coming to a standstill and people having to manage with the food gathered and stored during the summer months.

Fortunately, the clear mountain air and the simple diet keep the Garhwalis free from most diseases, and help them recover from the more common ailments. The greatest dangers come from unexpected disasters, such as an accident with an axe or scythe, or an attack by a wild animal. A few years back, several Manjari children and old women were killed by a man-eating leopard. The leopard was finally killed by the villagers who hunted it down with spears and axes. But the leopard that sometimes prowls round the village at night looking for a stray dog or goat slinks away at the approach of a human.

I do not see the leopard, but at night I am woken by a rumbling and thumping on the roof. I wake Gajadhar and ask him what is happening.

'It is only a bear,' he says.

'Is it trying to get in?'

'No, it's been in the cornfield and now it's after the pumpkins on the roof.'

A little later, when we look out of the small window, we see a black bear making off like a thief in the night, a large pumpkin held securely to his chest.

At the approach of winter when snow covers the higher mountains, the brown and black Himalayan bears descend to lower altitudes in search of food. Because they are short-sighted and suspicious of anything that moves, they can be dangerous; but, like most wild animals, they will avoid men if they can and are aggressive only when accompanied by their cubs.

Gajadhar advises me to run downhill if chased by a bear. He says that bears find it easier to run uphill than downhill.

I am not interested in being chased by a bear, but the following night, Gajadhar and I stay up to try and prevent the bear from depleting his cornfield. We take up our position on a highway promontory of rock, which gives us a clear view of the moonlit field.

A little after midnight, the bear comes down to the edge of the field but he is suspicious and has probably smelt us. He is, however, hungry; and so, after standing up as high as possible on his hind legs and peering about to see if the field is empty, he comes cautiously out of the forest and makes his way towards the corn.

When about halfway, his attention is suddenly attracted by some Buddhist prayer-flags which have been strung up recently between two small trees by a band of wandering Tibetans. On spotting the flags, the bear gives a little grunt of disapproval and begins to move back into the forest; but the fluttering of the little flags is a puzzle that he feels he must make out (for a bear is one of the most inquisitive animals); so after a few backward steps, he again stops and watches them.

Not satisfied with this, he stands on his hind legs looking at the flags, first at one side and then at the other. Then seeing that they do not attack him and so does not appear dangerous; he makes his way right up to the flags taking only two or three steps at a time and having a good look before each advance. Eventually, he moves confidently up to the flags and pulls them all down. Then, after careful examination of the flags, he moves into the field of corn.

But Gajadhar has decided that he is not going to lose any more corn, so he starts shouting, and the rest of the village wakes up and people come out of their houses beating drums and empty kerosene tins.

Deprived of his dinner, the bear makes off in a bad temper. He runs downhill and at a good speed too; and I am glad that I am not in his path just then. Uphill or downhill, an angry bear is best given a very wide berth.

For Gajadhar, impatient to know the result of his army entrance examination, the following day is a trial of his patience.

First, we hear that there has been a landslide and that the postman cannot reach us. Then, we hear that although there has been a landslide, the postman has already passed the spot in safety. Another alarming rumour has it that the postman disappeared with the landslide. This is soon denied. The postman is safe. It was only the mailbag that disappeared.

And then, at two in the afternoon, the postman turns up. He tells us that there was indeed a landslide but that it took place on someone else's route. Apparently, a mischievous urchin who passed him on the way was responsible for all the rumours. But we suspect the postman of having something to do with them…

Gajadhar has passed his examination and will leave with me in the morning. We have to be up early in order to reach Lansdowne before dark. But Gajadhar's mother insists on celebrating her son's success by feasting her friends and neighbours. There is a partridge (a present from a neighbour who had decided that Gajadhar will make a fine husband for his daughter), and two chickens: rich fare for folk whose normal diet consists mostly of lentils, potatoes and onions.

After dinner, there are songs, and Gajadhar's mother sings of the homesickness of those who are separated from their loved ones and their home in the hills. It is an old Garhwali folk-song:

> 'Oh, mountain-swift, you are from my father's home;
> Speak, oh speak, in the courtyard of my parents,
> My mother will hear you; She will send my brother to fetch me.
> A grain of rice alone in the cooking pot cries,
> "I wish I could get out!"
> Likewise I wonder: "Will I ever reach my father's house?"'

The hookah is passed round and stories are told. Tales of ghosts and demons mingle with legends of ancient kings and heroes. It is almost midnight by the time the last guest has gone. Chakradhar approaches me as I am about to retire for the night.

'Will you come again?' he asks.

'Yes, I'll come again,' I reply. 'If not next year, then the year after. How many years are left before you finish school?'

'Four.'

'Four years. If you walk ten miles a day for four years, how many miles will that make?'

'Four thousand and six hundred miles,' says Chakradhar after a moment's thought, 'but we have two months' holiday each year. That means I'll walk about 12,000 miles in four years.'

The moon has not yet risen. Lanterns swing in the dark.

The lanterns flit silently over the hillside and go out one by one. This Garhwali day, which is just like any other day in the hills, slips quietly into the silence of the mountains.

I stretch myself out on my cot. Outside the small window the sky is brilliant with stars. As I close my eyes, someone brushes against the lime tree, brushing its leaves; and the fresh fragrance of limes comes to me on the night air, making the moment memorable for all time.

THE NIGHT THE ROOF BLEW OFF

We are used to sudden storms, up here on the first range of the Himalayas. The old building in which we live has, for more than a hundred years, received the full force of the wind as it sweeps across the hills from the east.

We'd lived in the building for more than ten years without a disaster. It had even taken the shock of a severe earthquake. As my granddaughter Dolly said, 'It's difficult to tell the new cracks from the old!'

It's a two-storey building, and I live on the upper floor with my family: my three grandchildren and their parents. The roof is made of corrugated tin sheets, the ceiling of wooden boards. That's the traditional Mussoorie roof.

Looking back at the experience, it was the sort of thing that should have happened in a James Thurber story, like the dam that burst or the ghost who got in. But I wasn't thinking of Thurber at the time, although a few of his books were among the many I was trying to save from the icy rain pouring into my bedroom.

Our roof had held fast in many a storm, but the wind that night was really fierce. It came rushing at us with a high-pitched, eerie wail. The old roof groaned and protested. It took a battering for several hours while the rain lashed against the windows and the lights kept coming and going.

There was no question of sleeping, but we remained in bed for warmth and comfort. The fire had long since gone out, as the chimney had collapsed, bringing down a shower of sooty rainwater.

After about four hours of buffeting, the roof could take it no longer. My bedroom faces east, so my portion of the roof was the first to go.

The wind got under it and kept pushing until, with a ripping, groaning sound, the metal sheets shifted and slid off the rafters, some of them dropping with claps like thunder on to the road below.

So that's it, I thought. Nothing worse can happen. As long as the ceiling stays on, I'm not getting out of bed. We'll collect our roof in the morning.

Icy water splashing down on my face made me change my mind in a hurry. Leaping from the bed, I found that much of the ceiling had gone, too. Water was pouring on my open typewriter as well as on the bedside radio and bed cover.

Picking up my precious typewriter (my companion for forty years), I stumbled into the front sitting room (and library), only to find a similar situation there. Water was pouring through the slats of the wooden ceiling, raining down on the open bookshelves.

By now I had been joined by the children, who had come to my rescue. Their section of the roof hadn't gone as yet. Their parents were struggling to close a window against the driving rain.

'Save the books!' shouted Dolly, the youngest, and that became our rallying cry for the next hour or two.

Dolly and her brother Mukesh picked up armfuls of books

and carried them into their room. But the floor was awash, so the books had to be piled on their beds. Dolly was helping me gather some of my papers when a large field rat jumped on to the desk in front of her. Dolly squealed and ran for the door.

'It's all right,' said Mukesh, whose love of animals extends even to field rats. 'It's only sheltering from the storm.'

Big brother Rakesh whistled for our dog, Tony, but Tony wasn't interested in rats just then. He had taken shelter in the kitchen, the only dry spot in the house.

Two rooms were now practically roofless, and we could see the sky lit up by flashes of lightning.

There were fireworks indoors, too, as water spluttered and crackled along a damaged wire. Then the lights went out altogether.

Rakesh, at his best in an emergency, had already lit two kerosene lamps. And by their light we continued to transfer books, papers, and clothes to the children's room.

We noticed that the water on the floor was beginning to subside a little.

'Where is it going?' asked Dolly.

'Through the floor,' said Mukesh. 'Down to the flat below!'

Cries of concern from our downstairs neighbours told us that they were having their share of the flood.

Our feet were freezing because there hadn't been time to put on proper footwear. And besides, shoes and slippers were awash by now. All chairs and tables were piled high with books. I hadn't realized the extent of my library until that night!

The available beds were pushed into the driest corner of the children's room, and there, huddled in blankets and quilts, we spent the remaining hours of the night while the storm continued.

Towards morning the wind fell, and it began to snow. Through the door to the sitting room, I could see snowflakes drifting through the gaps in the ceiling, settling on picture-frames. Ordinary things like a glue bottle and a small clock took on a certain beauty when covered with soft snow.

Most of us dozed off.

When dawn came, we found the windowpanes encrusted with snow and icicles. The rising sun struck through the gaps in the ceiling and turned everything golden. Snow crystals glistened on the empty bookshelves. But the books had been saved.

Rakesh went out to find a carpenter and tinsmith, while the rest of us started putting things in the sun to dry. By evening we'd put much of the roof back on.

It's a much-improved roof now, and we look forward to the next storm with confidence!